MELISSA ALLRED

Widows Ranch

Preface

She wasn't young anymore, she thought, as she looked over the flower draped casket, towards the other mourners; who were all braving the cold rain, some with umbrellas; while others stood hunched against the wet and cold. She realized at that moment, that life had seemingly flown past her, while she thought she was living. But now in the middle of a cemetery surrounded by the headstones of all who had lived before, she realized that she never truly lived. It was as if the last forty-years of her life had been a short breath of time. Her broken heart matched the dark bleak February sky. A foreign feeling began to wrap its icy fingers like tentacles around her throat as she gasped through her sobs. She was now alone in the world. The minister finished his somber remarks with a prayer, and dismissed the crowd. Everyone began the slow process back to their vehicles. Some stopping to hug her and give their last sympathies. And then she was left standing alone. Her face wet from grief and the slow steady drizzle. "Why does it always rain during funerals?" She thought. The car she road in took her back to her own home. There wasn't anyone there to greet her. She turned the key in the lock and went inside.

The Funeral

Doris sat on the bed she had shared with her husband, Robert, for many years. His side now lay empty, except for a pair of pajamas he had left there the morning he passed away. Sitting alone on her side, that familiar icy feeling crept up her spine, and she shuddered. The clock on her bedside table read 11:42 p.m. She rubbed her swollen eyes, sighed, and stood up. Sleeping alone in the empty space between the two pillows felt unbearable.

She left the cold bedroom and moved into the dark living room, draping herself in the afghan blanket her mother had made for her thirtieth birthday. Settling into her chair, she leaned back and closed her eyes, letting the day's events flood her mind.

The funeral blurred into black umbrellas, rain-soaked coats, and muffled condolences. The steady patter of rain on the canvas overhead melded with the somber eulogies, creating a melancholy symphony. She stood by the casket, watching the procession of grief, feeling both disconnected and overwhelmed. It wasn't just the person they were gathered to mourn that she had lost; it was the life she had allowed to slip through her fingers.

Memories flickered past her like pages fluttering in a storm—moments of joy and sorrow, choices made and missed, love found and lost. Each memory served as a reminder of what could have been. The rain seemed to mirror her tears, each drop a testament to her regrets and unfulfilled dreams.

As the final words were spoken and the mourners dispersed, a chilling sense of isolation surrounded her. Left standing alone in the rain, the cold seeping through her clothes felt weak compared to the ice settling in her heart. The weight of being truly alone, with no one to anchor her, tightened its grip, making it hard to breathe.

The world felt unreal, as though she were watching it through a veil of rain and tears. The future stretched before her, undefined and daunting. The funeral marked the end of one chapter and the beginning of another, filled with uncertainty but also a faint glimmer of hope. Could this solitude and regret be a catalyst for change, a new beginning? Only time would tell.

Five weeks after the funeral, Doris sat across from a job recruiter at a dark chestnut desk, her legs bouncing in rhythm with her racing heartbeat. Her blood pulsed loudly in her ears. Robert hadn't left her with a comfortable inheritance, and now she needed to return to work just to make ends meet.

"Ms. Alan, I'm sorry, but I can't seem to find the right fit for someone your age who hasn't worked in 20 years," the recruiter began. "I understand you have clerical experience and are open to working as a grocery store cashier. But right now, the only positions I can find for you are as a greeter or maybe a hostess at Hurley's Steak House. The pay for both is, well, let's just say it's less than ideal. From what you've told me, you need at least thirty-five to forty thousand a year just to scrape by, and these jobs won't bring in more than eighteen thousand."

Doris struggled to focus on what Belinda Evans, the employment recruiter, said. Her head pounded, and she felt flushed—she had forgotten to take her blood pressure medication before leaving that morning. Anxiety gnawed at her. Robert had been the breadwinner, and his income as a master plumber allowed Doris to enjoy her hobbies and spend time with friends. But his sudden death revealed financial strains she hadn't anticipated. The life insurance was barely enough, and with unpaid bills piling up, she now faced selling their beloved home to avoid foreclosure.

"I understand," Doris replied, her voice cracking as she fought back tears. She stood, shaking Belinda's hand with a polite but strained smile. "I'll think it over and call you tomorrow. Thank you." Exiting the office, she squinted in the bright sunlight, momentarily blinded as she stumbled over a young man's feet.

"Oh my goodness, excuse me!" she exclaimed, her cheeks flushed with embarrassment.

The young man, probably in his late thirties or early forties, tipped his cowboy hat and apologized, steadying her. "No need to apologize, ma'am. I hope you're okay?"

"I'm fine, thank you," Doris reassured him, though her pride was more bruised than anything. The young man, Cody Haul, offered a friendly smile and handed her his business card. Tall, dark, and handsome, he reminded her of Robert in his younger days. "I'm not selling anything, ma'am, but if you need anything at all, please feel free to call me." His card listed him as a realtor and investor, with only his email and website and no company name.

"Thank you, Mr. Haul. I'll be in touch soon," she said, pocketing the card with a mix of confusion and curiosity. As she walked to her car, emotions she hadn't fully processed surged forward, spilling over as soon as she was safely inside.

Back at home, Doris sat at her kitchen bar, turning the business card over in her fingers—a tangible link to a lifeline she hadn't expected. She flipped the card back and forth, considering her next steps. Her computer glowed softly on the counter, displaying a blog post she had found on Cody Haul's website. The article discussed navigating financial decisions after a significant loss, echoing her situation in ways that felt both painful and reassuring.

The blog outlined five essential steps to consider before making financial decisions after a partner's death. It warned against making choices hastily, driven by grief instead of careful thought. Most helpful to Doris was the advice on consulting a financial advisor—someone to guide her through the maze of decisions ahead with a steady hand.

It felt as though the article had been written just for her, describing her situation almost exactly. The thought that she might need to sell the home she had shared with Robert felt overwhelming, a stark reminder of the financial reality she now faced alone. The house held so many memories, a testament to a life shared, and the thought of leaving it behind felt almost unbearable.

Doris and Robert had never had children—a decision that had seemed reasonable at the time but now left her feeling isolated in her grief. Her own family had passed, and her ties to Robert's family were tenuous at best, limited to a few nieces and nephews she barely knew. In this difficult moment, she felt as though she had no one to turn to for support or advice.

The thought crossed her mind that meeting Cody might not have been a coincidence. "Maybe God meant for us to meet," she murmured, a small thread of hope appearing in her voice for the first time in weeks.

Taking a deep breath that felt like a step toward a new beginning, she picked up her phone. Her fingers, steadier now, dialed Cody Haul's number. As it rang, a blend of anxiety and anticipation filled her chest. This call might be her first step in navigating an uncertain future—a small beacon of hope in the overwhelming darkness of her grief.

Cody's voice answered, "This is Cody…"

"Hello, Mr. Haul, this is Doris—the woman you tripped this morning," she said, a hint of humor in her voice.

After a brief pause, Cody replied, "Yes, ma'am, I remember. And you're still okay? I am sorry about that," he said, sounding sincere.

"Yes, I'm fine," she chuckled. "I'm just messing with you. I called to make an appointment. I was a bit distracted this morning because, well… I'm in a bit of a pickle, and I'm hoping you might help me figure things out."

Cody sounded happy to help. "I'm glad you called. Let me check my calendar… Alright, I have next Thursday at 2:30 open. Does that work?"

"Yes, that works," she replied, relieved not to have to wait too long. "Thank you, Mr. Haul. I'll see you then." They hung up, and Doris felt a small surge of confidence. She put the job search on hold, calling Belinda to let her know she needed a few more days to decide. With a renewed sense of purpose, she turned to the neglected laundry piling up in the corner. It wasn't a task she enjoyed, but today, it felt like a good distraction.

As Doris sorted through the laundry, her mind drifted to her upcoming meeting with Cody. The mundane task, which she usually found tedious, now offered a welcome distraction from her swirling thoughts and fears. Each piece of clothing she loaded into the machine seemed to lighten her burden, making a little more room for cautious optimism.

The days leading up to the meeting passed slowly, filled with moments of apprehension and unexpected flashes of resolve. Doris gathered all the documents Cody might need—bank statements, mortgage information,

Robert's life insurance policy, and a list of monthly expenses. Sorting through these details was sobering, confronting her with the stark reality of her finances. But it also gave her a sense of purpose. For the first time since Robert's passing, she felt as though she was beginning to take control of her life again.

Finally, Thursday arrived. Doris dressed carefully, choosing one of her business suits. She looked at herself in the mirror and took a deep breath to steady her nerves. The reflection staring back held determination, tinged with vulnerability.

The drive to Cody's office passed in a blur of green lights and familiar streets, her mind racing with what she would say, how Cody might react, and the different outcomes their meeting might lead to.

Cody greeted her with a warm smile, the same easy expression he'd worn when they first met. His office was bright and welcoming, with a large desk and two comfortable chairs in front of it. He motioned for her to sit, and as she did, Doris felt her tension begin to ease. Cody's demeanor was professional yet compassionate, creating a sense of trust and openness.

"I appreciate you taking the time to see me, Mr. Haul," Doris began, her voice steadier than she'd expected. "I'm not sure where to start, but I guess the truth is the best place."

Cody nodded warmly. "Please, call me Cody—'Mr. Haul' sounds too formal between friends." He smiled. "We're here to find solutions together, so take your time. I'm here to listen."

Doris shared everything—from the shock of Robert's sudden passing to the unsettling discovery of their financial situation and her fear of losing the home they had built together. Cody listened intently, his expression focused and compassionate, occasionally jotting down notes.

When Doris finished, Cody leaned back in his chair, looking thoughtful. "First, Doris, let me say how sorry I am for your loss. And thank you for trusting me with your story. I believe we can find a way through this. It won't be easy, and there will be some tough decisions, but you're not alone in this."

They discussed several options, from refinancing her mortgage to possibly selling the house and downsizing. Cody also suggested ways to stretch her resources and potentially bring in extra income.

By the end of the meeting, Doris felt as though a weight had lifted. Many uncertainties remained, but now she had a plan—a path forward. Cody had offered not just professional advice but genuine understanding and support.

As she drove home, the world seemed a little less daunting, the future a bit brighter. Doris realized that while the road ahead was uncertain, she was no longer navigating it alone. And for the first time in weeks, she allowed herself to feel a cautious hope about what lay ahead.

Something Different

"Come on! It'll be so much fun," Susan Reese urged. Doris gave her a look of doubt. Susan, her longtime friend and partner in what they called their "shenanigans," was trying to convince her to take a weekend vacation to a local ranch for single women—a boot camp for learning the "Art of Cowboying."

"Is that what they're calling it?" Doris smirked.

"Yes, it's their gimmick! And look how cute the cabins are," Susan gushed, showing her a picture of the view from the room. The windows had charming country curtains, and flower boxes were full of vibrant spring flowers.

"Ugh!" Doris sighed. "I don't know, Susan! I have so much to do right now, and I don't think I have the time."

"Now, Doris, I know you don't have anything pressing. You've been wasting away in that house alone for weeks! What's so important that you can't take three days for fresh country air and some good food? Look at this," she pointed to the menu in the brochure. "Country-fried steak and eggs on Friday, and bacon and grits with cereal on Saturday for breakfast!" Susan squealed like a schoolgirl, and Doris felt her stomach rumble at the thought. It had been a while since she'd had a meal like that.

Her mother used to make a feast on Saturday mornings just like that. It was a wonder she'd kept her slim figure growing up. She and Robert used to go on breakfast dates at a local restaurant that specialized in country-style dishes whenever his schedule allowed. Later, as work got busier, they had to settle for a few outings each month. The memory brought fresh tears to her eyes, but she quickly wiped them away before Susan noticed.

Susan kept talking about the ranch's amenities and the different "chores" they'd be doing. Doris finally interjected, "Wait, so we're paying $150 a night to work as ranch hands? Do they want us to pay to do their jobs and call it a vacation? This sounds like a scam, Susan!"

Susan paused, a little taken aback, then patted her hand. "It's okay, love; you don't have to pay a dime. I'm covering us both. A little work will do your attitude some good. Trust me, I know exactly what you need, and this is it. So pack your bags, sister—we leave in two days!"

Doris was surprised by her friend's firm tone. In all their years together, Susan had never spoken to her like that. Eyes wide and mouth open, she gave Susan a shocked look.

"Well, okay, yes ma'am," she said, saluting her like a soldier.

Both women stared at each other before bursting into laughter and hugging.

Susan's insistence and enthusiasm marked a turning point for Doris, nudging her out of her comfort zone and into a potentially healing experience. Despite her initial reluctance, the idea of a weekend at a ranch for single women to learn "cowboying" skills offered an intriguing escape from the solitude and routine that had filled her life since Robert's passing.

The laughter shared between Doris and Susan, a testament to their deep bond, was a balm to Doris' heavy heart. It reminded her that joy still existed in the world, waiting to be rediscovered—even in unexpected places like a ranch that blended work and relaxation under the guise of a vacation.

Susan's insistence, coupled with her offer to cover the costs, left Doris with little room to refuse. The thought of stepping away from her grief, even just for a weekend, began to feel not only necessary but essential. "Maybe Susan is right," Doris thought, a glimmer of anticipation surfacing. "Maybe what I need is to get away, to breathe differently, even if it means paying to do chores on a ranch!"

In the two days before their departure, Doris found herself caught up in a whirlwind of preparations. She packed her bags with clothes she imagined would suit a ranch—jeans she hadn't worn in years, comfortable boots, and flannel shirts. With each item she folded, a sense of adventure began to rekindle, a feeling she thought had faded with Robert's passing.

As they set off, the open road stretched before them, promising new experiences and memories. The drive to the ranch was filled with Susan's chatter about the activities they'd try, from horseback riding to learning how to lasso. Doris listened, her skepticism slowly fading as the cityscape gave way to rolling hills and open fields.

Arriving at the ranch, the quaint cabins and the beauty of the surrounding nature struck Doris unexpectedly. The air was fresh, filled with the scent of wildflowers and freshly cut grass. The sight of the cabins, decorated with charming country touches and vibrant flower boxes, brought a smile to Doris' face—the first genuine one in what felt like forever.

The weekend passed in a blur of activity. Doris found herself immersed in the daily routines of ranch life, each chore a new experience that tested her physical and emotional limits. From early morning wake-ups for country breakfasts that tasted of nostalgia to evenings around a campfire under a blanket of stars, she shared stories and laughter with other women also searching for something they felt was missing.

The work, far from the "scam" Doris had initially thought, turned out to be strangely fulfilling. Something was grounding in the physical effort and the tangible results, a feeling she hadn't experienced in a long time. Lying in her cabin on the last night, exhaustion mixed with contentment, she realized Susan had been right. This retreat—a brief escape into the world of cowboying—had given her a break from her grief and a glimpse into a life still worth living.

As the weekend came to a close, Doris and Susan packed their bags, their laughter echoing in the cabin one last time. The drive home was reflective, with Doris gazing out the window at the passing landscape, emotions swirling within her. She felt renewed—not only from the change in scenery but from the realization that she could still find joy, that life held possibilities waiting to be explored.

"Thank you," Doris said softly, her voice filled with gratitude. "This weekend was exactly what I needed."

Susan simply squeezed her hand, their friendship a steady anchor in the ever-changing tides of life.

As they neared home, Doris felt a new determination take root within her. The journey through grief wasn't over, but now she knew she didn't have to walk it alone. And perhaps, just maybe, it was time to start looking forward—to new adventures and unwritten chapters waiting ahead.

The following morning, Doris woke up stiff and sore from the weekend, but it was a good kind of pain—a reminder that she was alive and that her heart was still working. Sitting up in bed, she felt a new vigor she hadn't experienced in years. Life with Robert had been happy but often felt predictable and routine. Sundays meant church, followed by Robert's nap after lunch. Doris would watch TV while crocheting or play solitaire on her phone. Mondays were Robert's busiest days; he'd leave early for work and wouldn't return until late, meaning they didn't eat dinner until after seven-thirty most evenings.

On Tuesdays, Robert commuted out of town to the office he co-owned with a colleague he'd met in school. They split the work week evenly, with Robert covering Tuesday through Thursday and his partner, Jim, taking Friday through Sunday. They had a few employees, but work in Bardwell was often slow, so Robert contracted jobs in neighboring towns as well. As he grew older, managing the demands of his job became harder, and he eventually sold his share of the business to Jim's apprentice.

After Robert's passing, Doris realized that their finances had been stretched tighter than she'd known. They'd refinanced their mortgage multiple times, sometimes to fund Robert's work vehicle repairs or to buy new equipment. The last refinance, a few years before Robert's death, left $150,000 to be paid back. Without Robert's income, Doris couldn't cover the $1,500 mortgage and her other expenses. She cut costs wherever possible—limiting grocery shopping to once a month, stopping trash service, and canceling cable, but she kept the internet for the essentials.

Despite these cuts, she was still a thousand dollars short each month. The only logical choices were to sell her home or return to work, even though she hadn't been employed in twenty years. Now sixty-six, with only a high school diploma, her job prospects were limited. She'd worked at a local grocery store early in her marriage and later as a bill collector at the nearby hospital, but she'd left when Robert's income allowed her to stay home and focus on her household and hobbies.

Doris had filled her time with volunteer work and met her best friend, Susan, at the "Society for Preservation," a club dedicated to protecting historic homes in the area. They quickly became inseparable, and soon the community knew them as "Double Trouble." Together, they organized events at church and rallied support for local causes. When Robert passed, her friends and church family surrounded her with love, flowers, cards, and home-cooked meals, a kindness she cherished.

But now, facing financial strain, Doris began to withdraw from the community activities she once loved. Susan, recognizing the signs of isolation, devised the plan for their weekend retreat to give Doris a much-needed break. And it had worked. Doris was grateful for Susan's care and her insight into the struggles of widowhood.

Stretching her arms toward the ceiling, Doris swung her legs out of bed, reached for her glasses, and glanced at the bedside clock—7:34 a.m. She rarely slept so late, but the weekend had left her exhausted. Yawning, she rose, craving coffee.

After a quick cup and a shower, Doris prepared to tackle some unfinished business. Cody had left her a voicemail over the weekend with several ideas to consider: renting out her home to a roommate, selling it, or fully renting it out while she found a smaller place to live. Each option had its pros and cons, and Doris wasn't certain which route was best.

If she sold the home, Cody estimated she could make around $500,000—enough to cover her debts and have some left over for investing. She could then live modestly on her Social Security and survivor benefits, with the option to work if she chose. Alternatively, if she rented the house, she might generate enough income to cover her monthly expenses, but it would require finding affordable housing for herself, such as a small efficiency or single-wide trailer in a nearby park.

As Doris sipped her coffee, the warmth of the mug in her hands mirrored the warmth that the weekend with Susan had rekindled in her spirit. The ranch had been more than an escape; it was a reminder of her resilience and her capacity for joy amid sorrow. Standing quietly in her kitchen, she realized that the choice before her wasn't just about finances; it was about setting a new direction for her life.

Setting her coffee down, Doris picked up the phone and dialed Cody.

"Cody, it's Doris. I've been thinking about our conversation before the weekend, and I'm still torn," she began, her voice steady but carrying the weight of indecision.

Cody listened patiently, offering thoughtful responses to her concerns. He reminded her to consider not only the financial implications but also her quality of life and emotional well-being.

"You have options, Doris," he advised. "Each has its pros and cons, but remember, this decision is about what's best for you in the long run."

After the call, Doris sat in silence, letting his words sink in. Slowly, a sense of clarity emerged. Selling the house, as difficult as it would be emotionally, seemed like the fresh start she needed—a chance to rebuild her life on her own terms. She could picture herself in a small, cozy efficiency filled with new memories, a simpler but peaceful place to call her own.

Feeling her resolve solidify, Doris called Cody back, her voice carrying a new sense of determination. "Cody, let's go ahead with selling the house. I'm ready for a new chapter."

"Wow! Okay, then," Cody replied, a bit surprised. "I honestly didn't expect to hear back so soon. Are you certain?"

"Yes," Doris confirmed. "It's not easy, but I need a fresh start. The weekend showed me that I have to find my own path forward. I can't do that tied to what Robert and I built together. It's time to take the bull by the horns and make a go of something different."

"Well, alright, then," Cody said. "I'll get to work on listing your property. Swing by my office when you can; I'll need a spare key. I'll arrange for an appraiser and have photos taken. Given the current market, I think we can sell within four weeks. I'm confident we can ask for $500,000, maybe a bit more. After closing costs, and depending on any necessary repairs, you'll likely clear between $350,000 and $420,000. Enough to pay off your mortgage and have a solid amount left over to start fresh. How does that sound?"

"That sounds reasonable, Cody. I'm putting my trust in you," Doris replied with a hint of relief.

After they hung up, Doris took a long, reflective look around her kitchen and living room. Soon, every memory-filled corner would need to be packed up. Downsizing from her current space to a small 350-square-foot efficiency would require letting go of many belongings, which was both daunting and liberating.

With newfound resolve, she began carefully taking down her collectibles from the shelves, setting them on the kitchen counter. She'd need boxes for packing, and many items would have to be donated. As she surveyed the room, filled with the remnants of a lifetime, the task felt monumental. Yet, underneath the sadness, there was a glimmer of excitement—a sense of liberation in distilling her life down to its essentials, preparing herself for the next chapter.

Doris called Susan with the news, and together they made plans to meet the following weekend to start packing.

As the rooms slowly emptied, the reality of her decision settled in. There were moments of doubt, fleeting thoughts of whether she was making the right choice, but she remembered the resolve that had solidified during her call with Cody. This wasn't just about finances; it was about reclaiming her life.

With the house officially on the market and her belongings pared down to the essentials, Doris felt a profound readiness for whatever lay ahead. She envisioned her new space not as a limitation but as a blank canvas, a place for new memories and fresh beginnings. The efficiency apartment, though modest, would be all hers—a reflection of the woman she was becoming in this new chapter of her life.

In the quiet of what would soon no longer be her home, Doris allowed herself a moment of reflection. The journey from grief to determination had been unexpected, a path she'd navigated with the support of friends like Susan and professionals like Cody. She realized that while she was leaving behind a house filled with memories, she was stepping into a future where she could build new ones, grounded in self-reliance and the courage to embrace change.

The days passed slowly as Doris prepared for her move. She shopped for a few pieces of new decor to make the apartment truly hers, and Susan often stopped by with coffee or lunch. As Doris waited for an offer on the house, she visited nearby apartments and eventually found one in a neighboring city close to her church and familiar places. It felt just right, so she signed a lease.

Four weeks after listing the house, a young couple made an offer for $550,000—above asking price. Doris was thrilled to accept it. After a few repairs, she cleared $302,000. She invested $10,000 with Cody's guidance and took the rest to the bank.

With the help of some teenage boys from her church, Doris moved into her new apartment in Ennis, a small but inviting space. It felt like a blank canvas, waiting to be filled with new memories and experiences, all of it hers to design.

A New Normal

Doris woke up in her old bed that first morning but in a new environment. The thrill of starting fresh energized her as she arranged her small kitchen, placing her pots, pans, and dishes into their cabinets. Realizing she'd missed breakfast and the day was warming up, she decided to shower and head to the grocery store. Bardwell, her former neighborhood, was familiar and comforting, so she arrived there.

With a list in hand, Doris began filling her shopping cart. As music played over the store's intercom, she thought about the times she'd shopped for two. Now, on a new, tighter budget, she frequently checked her calculator to avoid overspending. While focusing on her list, she suddenly felt a tap on her shoulder. Turning, she saw a familiar face.

"Look what the cat dragged in! How are you, *Shugga?*" exclaimed Lisa Harrell, an old school friend. Surprised but pleased, Doris hugged her tightly.

"Oh my goodness, Lisa! I haven't seen you in forever! You look like you haven't aged a day. What's your secret?" Doris asked with genuine curiosity.

"Stop it, you!" Lisa laughed. "No secret here—just a bit of help from my plastic surgeon! But you're the one who looks amazing." Doris blushed, not believing it herself. Lisa had always been the beauty everyone admired.

"So, how's Lonnie doing these days?" Doris asked.

Lisa's eyes grew misty. "He's been fighting prostate cancer since last March. The doctors think he's in the clear, but we have a few more rounds of chemo before they're certain."

Doris' expression softened, and she said with empathy, "I knew y'all were going through a rough time, but I'll be praying for God's grace in this journey and for complete healing."

Lisa, who had married shortly after Doris in 1963, had been a bridesmaid at Doris' wedding. They'd shared several double dates before Lisa and Lonnie moved to California for his work at a shipping yard. Time had flown, but they'd kept in touch through letters and social media.

Hugging her friend again, Lisa said, "I was heartbroken to hear about Robert. He was such a good man. He always had a quick remark for me….but he was genuinely a good guy. Lonnie and I were both devastated by the news. Are you doing okay? Do you need anything?"

Doris smiled warmly. "Thank you, Lisa. I'm getting by. I sold the house recently and moved into an apartment in Ennis. You should come by sometime. Be my first guest!"

"Why sure *Shuggs*! I'd be delighted to visit. Is six o'clock okay? I'll bring some red wine. We can do some catching up." Lisa suggested.

Smiling, Doris accepted, looking forward to an evening of reminiscing. She finished her shopping, adding a chocolate cake to her cart before heading home to tidy up. Her space was small, so it didn't take long to make it presentable. She pushed boxes aside and covered them with a blanket, arranging her most cherished items on the built-in shelves. By six o'clock, Doris was exhausted but happy with her work. She had bought new curtains and a new comforter for her old bed.

The spaghetti was almost ready when her doorbell rang. Lisa arrived punctually, wine in hand, and Doris welcomed her into the cozy apartment. She found her wine glasses in a box marked kitchen and poured them both a glass as they waited for the timer on the stove to signal that dinner was ready. They reminisced about old times, with Lisa admiring the simple details of Doris's new home, which made her feel better about her decision to move.

The dinner was delicious, and a second pour of wine with the chocolate cake hit the spot. By the time Lisa left, Doris felt pleasantly exhausted, ready to crash for the night.

Sometime later, Doris was startled awake by sirens. As she groggily opened her eyes, she heard loud knocking. Cracking her door open, she saw the commotion across the hall—a tall slender police officer standing on the other side, his back towards Doris. He was speaking to the female occupant inside. She could hear a child crying, and someone shouting in another unit next to her. It was unsettling, especially on her second night in the new apartment.

Back in bed, Doris glanced at the clock: 12:15 a.m. Though she struggled to fall asleep, the familiar icy realization of being alone settled into her stomach. She didn't know if this was the best idea after all. In her old neighborhood, her neighbors all knew each other, And there had never been any trouble with the police on her block. she eventually drifted off, but her dreams were turbulent. She dreamt that she was looking for Robert, only to find him reaching out his hand towards her, with fear in his eyes, as he dangled from a cliff, and she tried to scream as she watched him fall before she could grab him. Jerking awake at 4:25 a.m., drenched in sweat, she buried her face in her hands and wept. It was too early to be awake; the disturbance in the wee hours of the morning had caused her to be groggy. She felt queasy, too. She closed her eyes and soon could sleep again without more dreams.

When morning light filled her room, she felt the previous night's events lingering in her mind, a reminder of the unfamiliar life she was building alone, and facing a new day with less energy than the previous one, she decided that the chocolate cake and wine had been a tad too rich for her, especially right before bedtime. That, coupled with the night's events, had unsettled her. She felt dehydrated and depressed. This wasn't the best way to start out her second day as an independent woman.

Despite the unease, she pushed herself out of bed, determined to start the day. She made her way to the kitchen and prepared a light breakfast: green tea, known for its hydrating properties and gentle boost of energy as well as some cinnamon toast. Doris ate her meager breakfast, reflecting on the mix of excitement, anxiety, and lingering sadness she felt.

To ground herself, Doris set small goals for the day, deciding to finish unpacking the last few boxes left from her move. Organizing her new home, she hoped, would help the space feel truly hers. After lunch, she took a short walk around her new neighborhood, locating a nearby park and enjoying the peaceful scenery. She rested on a bench, watching young mothers with their children play on the playground. Feeling unexpectedly at ease, Doris decided to introduce herself to two of the mothers, Madison and Leah.

The sound of children's laughter and the day's warmth lifted her spirits. After a brief chat, she continued exploring her neighborhood, discovering a community garden and a quaint café she hoped would become her new favorite spot. She felt uplifted when she returned home, embracing the beauty of her new beginning.

That evening, Doris called her friend Susan to share her experiences of the day—and the previous night's unsettling events.

"I've never experienced anything like it before! And it put me on edge. Of course, the wine didn't help at all. I should have known better."Doris confessed, "But I just wasn't thinking...." she trailed off into thought.

Susan's support was unwavering, but she did have her own slight doubts about the events of the evening with the police. "Have you heard anything else from your neighbor regarding the incident?" She asked

"I haven't heard a peep or noise at all since. I'm hoping it was just a fluke. A one-off. Or something. You know, just a bad night. I've not allowed myself to linger on it too much."

Susan, ever supportive, replied, "If you feel unsafe there, maybe we can talk to the landlord and either get you moved to a different unit or something or even see if they will allow you to vacate the lease agreements with the circumstances. I hate to think you're uncomfortable, especially with your new journey. Let me know how I can help."

The conversation ended with Susan's plans to visit soon, bringing more housewarming gifts and the promise of shared moments.

Doris was extra cautious about revealing that she was living alone, doing small things to feel safer in her new space. She'd heard a tip on a YouTube video for single women living alone: by putting a pair of men's shoes outside the door to make it appear like someone else lived there. It sounded silly, but Doris was still learning how to be alone. She had married Robert straight out of high school and never had the opportunity to live by herself. The whole experience was new. And she was not always confident or comfortable about being on her own. She even found a YouTube video of an older man talking about construction projects, which she played as loud as she dared to mimic someone else being in the apartment.

It must have worked because Susan came by unexpectedly one evening, and her shocked and confused face spoke volumes about what she thought she heard. But there was no place to hide another person in such a small space, and once Doris explained herself, Susan laughed uncontrollably and had to hold onto the kitchen counter near the door.

"I swear, I thought you had a man in here! Lord have mercy; I was just about to get back in my car and leave. I thought you'd gotten yourself a new boyfriend…and I was gonna start snooping around to find out who this new mister might be…." She laughed some more, and Doris was beat red with embarrassment at the thought that Susan would suspect her of having an affair.

"Well, aren't you miss Goody Two Shoes?" She quipped back, annoyed at the thought that she might just up and forget about Robert so quickly. Her wedding ring still on her finger, Doris could not even fathom the thought of loving again.

"I'm sorry, " Susan said, gesturing towards Doris with her hands, "I didn't mean to offend you; I just didn't know what to think. Honestly, the ruse is actually really good. It sounds like there is someone else in here with you. It fooled even me! And I should have known better."

Doris playfully pushed Susan on her shoulder and said, "Of all the things, Susan, yes, you should have known." She had forgiven her friend, and they laughed even harder at the prospect of Doris entertaining a gentleman.

"So anyways, I'm sorry to just drop by unannounced like this, Susan said, breaking into their humorous moment. "But, I was actually on this side of town and saw a house in the older neighborhood slated for demolition. We must address the city council and determine what they want to keep it up.

Doris found herself drawn into the prospect of a new project that promised to reconnect her with the community and, perhaps, offer a sense of purpose. She listened as Susan continued.

"The club will need to convene and consider if it's worth the effort. It's really run down, but it was once one of the Belles of Ennis, a true darling during its heyday.

"I'll make some calls to the club and set up an emergency meeting." Doris offered.

Susan smiled gently. She knew her friend needed a job right now, something to keep her mind occupied during the days while she learned to live alone. Susan's experience of finding her way after her husband Bill had passed away lent to her experience and gave her empathy for what her friend was going through.

Susan was thirty-two when she became a widow. After Bill passed, she moved to Texas after living in Georgia with her close-knit family for support. She had a thriving career there, but losing her soulmate caused her to rethink her life. Because of her career, she was able to relocate easily.

Even though her mother begged her to move back home, she forged ahead, making her own way through the loneliness and fear of being alone. She found her strength through the connections she made along the way. Susan and Doris met through the Preservation Society.

She could see the same strength in Doris now. Though she needed a little nudge now and then, she knew that her friend would find her own way, too.

Before the meeting, Doris and Susan decided to gather as much information as possible about the house—its history, architectural significance, and any previous preservation efforts. They also took photographs to document its current state, intending to use these as part of their presentation to the club.

The agenda for the club meeting included a discussion on the house's historical value, potential strategies for its preservation, fundraising ideas, and the planning of an appeal to the city council. Doris had created a presentation, leveraging her recent experiences to demonstrate the house's significance to the community. With everyone called upon to attend, the meeting was set for a Friday afternoon at the local library.

The meeting day arrived, and Doris greeted the members: "Thank you, everyone, for coming on such short notice. As Susan and I mentioned, there's a house in the old neighborhood. We have given her the name "The Belle of Ennis. "The home is in danger of demolition. We believe it's a significant piece of our town's history." Susan passed folders to each member.

Margret Scott chimed in as she glanced over the photos. "Oh, I remember this house! My grandmother used to tell me stories about the grand parties held there. It's such a shame to think it could be torn down."

John Adams, one of the club's senior members, wasn't convinced and interjected, "What exactly are you proposing we do? Preservation is expensive, and from these photos, it looks like the house has seen better days."

"That's a fair point, John." Doris answered, "We're considering a few options—applying for historical grants, crowdfunding, maybe even approaching local businesses for sponsorship. But first, we need to convince the city council to delay the demolition".

John's wife, Helen offered her opinion: "I like the idea of crowdfunding. There's a lot of interest in local history these days. Perhaps we could also organize a public event to raise awareness and funds?"

Not convinced, John leaned back in his chair, arms folded. "There is no way we can find someone to match this part of the facade to the original on the other side. The unique roof, as well as the material and the craftsmanship to fix this, is going to be a headache, not to mention very expensive." John was a contractor by trade and an experienced architect, too. His contribution to the club was valued, and his words held a lot of weight. Everyone was looking at him now, concern etching their faces. Some were shaking their head in agreement.

Frank Middleton raised his hand now, and Doris recognized him; "Go ahead Frank." He stood up and asked "Are we prepared to take on the management of this property, though? Assuming we're successful in saving it, who's going to oversee its restoration and maintenance? John knows his stuff, and we all can see how dilapidated this building is. How long are we talking for this project? By the looks of it, this is more than a few months work."

Susan took the ball and replied "Another valid concern. We'd need to form a committee to manage the project, look into grants specifically for restoration, and possibly partner with preservation experts. It's a big commitment, but I believe it's doable with the right planning."

Margaret raised her hand and offered a solution: "What about reaching out to the local university's architecture department? They might be interested in taking on some of the work as a project. It could be beneficial for both parties."

"That's a brilliant suggestion, Margaret!" Susan replied with enthusiasm. "It could really help with some of the costs and get the younger generation involved in preservation efforts. As well as helping us solve the problem that John brought to the table."

Helen jumped in: "It sounds like we have a solid starting point. I think it's important we also prepare a detailed presentation for the city council, outlining the historical significance of the house and our proposed plans. Count me in for organizing the community event. I'll start putting together some ideas and a potential budget."

"Thank you Helen, for volunteering that part." Doris said smiling at her. It was good to see other members catching the spirit of the project.

Helen turned to her husband who still had his arms crossed; and nudged him gently.

"And I'll reach out to my contacts in construction and restoration. He offered. "Maybe we can get some initial estimates and advice on what we're looking at in terms of restoration" he said grudgingly.

But Doris and Susan weren't deterred by John's attitude. They both thanked him. Susan concluded the meeting by saying, "Thank you, everyone, for your enthusiasm and ideas. Seeing so much support for preserving our town's history is heartening. Let's meet again next week to consolidate our plans and set things in motion.

As Doris and Susan walked out of the library, Doris exclaimed, "This is wonderful! Everyone is on board. Now, if we can get the City's support, I really think we can save the Belle of Ennis!"

The Belle of Ennis

With everything in place, Doris and Susan requested a slot on the agenda for the upcoming city council meeting. Doris, although nervous, felt a surge of determination. She had rehearsed her presentation meticulously, highlighting the house's potential to enrich the community—not just as a relic of the past but as a vibrant part of the town's future.

On the day of the city council meeting, Doris and Susan arrived early, well-prepared with a thick binder of materials and backed by a crowd of supporters who gathered outside the council chambers. When Doris stood to speak before the council, a projector screen behind her displayed a majestic image of the Belle of Ennis in its prime. She felt the moment's weight—not only for the house but as a testament to how far she had come since Robert's passing. Clearing her throat, she began her presentation nervously and determinedly, glancing at Susan, who winked back.

"Ladies and Gentlemen of Council, thank you for this opportunity to speak. I stand here on behalf of the Society for Preservation and concerned citizens to discuss the fate of the Belle of Ennis, a historic gem that has graced our town for over a century. This house is more than just a structure; it's a testament to our town's history, architectural beauty, and cultural significance. Sadly, it now faces the threat of demolition to make way for new developments."

She clicked on the next slide, which showed the house's deterioration over the years.

"While it's true that the Belle of Ennis has seen better days, we believe its restoration can serve as a beacon of our town's commitment to preserving its heritage. We propose not only to save the house from demolition but to restore it to its former glory and transform it into a community heritage center. This center would educate future generations about our town's history and serve as a venue for community events, bringing together residents and visitors alike."

Doris then outlined preliminary plans for fundraising, grants, and community involvement, emphasizing the project's potential benefits to the town's cultural and economic landscape.

Council Member Johnson was the first to speak. "Ms. Alan, your passion for preserving our town's history is commendable. However, have you considered the financial implications of such a restoration project? How do you propose we fund this endeavor?"

"Thank you for the question, Councilman," Doris replied. "We've identified several funding sources, including historic preservation grants, crowdfunding, and potential sponsorship from local businesses. We also plan to host fundraising events to engage the community and raise awareness. While we understand the concerns about cost, we believe the long-term benefits to our town's cultural heritage and economy will far outweigh the initial investment."

"And what about the ongoing property maintenance once it's restored? Who will be responsible for that?" Council Member Watkins asked.

"That's a great question," Doris responded confidently. "We propose forming a non-profit organization dedicated to the maintenance and operation of the heritage center. We envision it becoming self-sustaining through event rentals, donations, and possibly a small entrance fee for tours, with all proceeds going toward the upkeep of the property."

"It's an ambitious project," Council Member Lee remarked, challenging her, "Do you have any estimates on visitor numbers and potential revenue it could generate?"

Doris was undeterred. She responded with determination, like a skilled tennis player volleying a shot back to her opponent: "Based on preliminary research and comparisons with similar heritage centers, we project a steady rise in visitor numbers, especially with educational programs and special events. As for revenue, we're working with local tourism experts to create detailed projections, which we'd be happy to share once finalized," she added, her confidence evident.

As Doris finished her presentation, the room was filled with consideration. The council members exchanged whispers, clearly intrigued by the proposal's potential.

The Council Chairman spoke with authority, and the room was so quiet you could hear a pin drop.

"Thank you, Ms. Alan, for a thorough presentation. You and the Society for Preservation have put significant thought into this proposal. We will need to review the details further and consider the financial aspects, but this is an intriguing project that merits serious consideration. We will deliberate and return with our decision. Thank you for bringing this to our attention."

Doris nodded, a sense of relief washing over her. Regardless of the outcome, she sparked a conversation about preservation and community heritage, bringing the plight of the Belle of Ennis into the town's awareness.

Outside City Hall, Susan hugged Doris. "I'm so proud of you! You hit that one out of the park."

John shook Doris' hand. "Congratulations! I'm confident the council members will vote to save the house. Be ready to put all your energy into it once things start moving—it'll be full steam ahead. Hope you're prepared."

Helen hugged her as well. "You did wonderfully! I'd vote for you in a second."

The others echoed their support before heading home one by one.

As the council members began their deliberations, Doris realized that regardless of the outcome, this effort marked a significant step in her journey of self-discovery and re-engagement with the world. She had moved from the solitude of grief to the forefront of a community effort, finding new purpose and connection along the way.

She offered a quick, silent prayer as she walked to her vehicle: "Lord, Your will be done, whatever it might be. I'm just praying that if this passes, You'll give me the strength and courage to see it through."

It didn't take long to hear back from City Hall with the approval, giving

Doris the green light to move forward with the project. She called Susan immediately.

Bursting with excitement and unable to contain her enthusiasm, she shouted into her speaker, "We got it!" as soon as Susan answered. Equally thrilled, Susan responded, "Oh my goodness, that's incredible news! I knew they couldn't resist your proposal. What are the next steps? When do we start?"

Doris replied, "They've given us the go-ahead to start the planning phase. Let's get together as soon as possible to map out our strategy. There's so much to do—fundraising, applying for grants, organizing community events for support, and, of course, the restoration plans themselves."

Susan, always Johhny on the Spot, suggested, "Let's call a meeting for this weekend. We can outline our plan and assign tasks. I'll start putting together a list of potential donors and grant opportunities. And maybe it's time to reach out to that architect friend of mine for an initial assessment of the house."

Doris, feeling a mix of relief and anticipation, agreed, "That sounds perfect, Susan. I'll draft the agenda for our meeting and email it to the members tonight. We should also consider a press release to announce the project to the community—it might help drum up support and attract volunteers."

Sensing Doris' slight overwhelmed, Susan reassured her, "Doris, we've got this. Look at how far we've come already. This house isn't just a building; it's a testament to our community's history and resilience. We will make it a place everyone in town can be proud of."

Heartened by Susan's words, Doris felt a renewed sense of purpose. "You're right, Susan. This is more than just a project; it's our chance to leave a lasting legacy. Let's bring the Belle of Ennis back to life."

With plans set in motion and the future looking brighter than ever, Doris and Susan ended their call, ready to embark on the next chapter of their journey, fueled by determination and the support of their community.

Resilience

Despite their progress, the Belle project faced unexpected challenges that tested the resolve and unity of the Club and the broader community.

Just as the restoration began to pick up momentum, a major setback occurred: a significant grant they had been counting on fell through. Originally intended to cover many restoration costs, the grant was suddenly redirected to a more urgent project after a natural disaster struck the state. Several Texas counties had been devastated by a wildfire, leading the governor to declare a state of emergency to release funds. This left the restoration project critically underfunded, with a gaping hole in the budget threatening to halt all progress.

When Doris received the call, it felt like the wind had been removed from her sails. She had been riding high on the community's momentum and support, but now the project was at risk. She couldn't fully process the news as she hung up the phone. Sitting down, she tried to gather her thoughts, but clarity eluded her. *Why couldn't she just focus?* she wondered.

Desperate for some perspective, Doris picked up her cell phone and called Susan, who was always supportive and optimistic in such situations.

"This is a setback," Susan offered, "but it's not the end. We've faced challenges before. Remember the bake sale fiasco? If we could get through that, we can get through this."

"Susan, that was a cakewalk—no pun intended—compared to this one!" Doris said, her tone a bit downcast.

Susan laughed at her friend's unintentional joke, glad Doris still had her sense of humor.

"Well, it wasn't much of a 'cakewalk' then, as I remember!" Susan replied, laughing so hard that tears came to her eyes as she recalled what they all lovingly called the "Bake Sale Fiasco," which time had transformed from tragedy into comedy.

During a pivotal time in the club's history—when they were raising funds to save a local park with historical significance—the Society for Preservation decided to host a community bake sale. The event, intended to raise funds and awareness for the park project, turned into an unexpected comedy of errors they could now laugh about. The team had meticulously planned every detail, from the variety of baked goods to the decorations that would make their stall irresistibly inviting. By leveraging her social media skills, Susan had built up significant anticipation online, promising an array of homemade treats.

The first snag came with a misprint in the local newspaper ad due to a communication mix-up. The bake sale was advertised to start at 10 a.m., though the correct start time was 8 a.m. This led to a slow start, with volunteers and baked goods all ready and waiting but barely a trickle of customers in sight.

Despite the forecast for clear skies, the weather was a fickle friend. By mid-morning, dark clouds rolled in just as the crowd began to pick up, bringing a sudden downpour that sent volunteers, baked goods, and decorations into a soggy disarray. The team scrambled to cover the tables with plastic sheets, but many baked goods didn't survive the storm.

To make matters worse, John, who had been tasked with setting up the tables and signage, realized too late that the measurements for the space were off. This resulted in a cramped, chaotic arrangement, barely accommodating all the baked goods. With the rain pouring down and everyone trying to save the pastries in time, an incident occurred that would become one of the most memorable moments of their lives.

In the scramble to salvage what they could from the rain, a misstep led to what would forever be known as the "Great Pie Incident." Many of their pie selection toppled off the table in a domino-like effect. One pie, in particular, was launched skyward, and as everyone rushed to cover the tables, it landed squarely on Frank's head, whipped cream dripping down his bewildered face. He didn't quite know what had happened, and everyone froze in shock.

Someone from the community snapped a photo and posted it on the town's Facebook page. While disheartening at the time, this spectacle became a humorous highlight for those who witnessed it—and later, for the team.

Feeling defeated, the team was ready to call it a day when the community's response surprised them. Word of the fiasco spread quickly, drawing more people out of curiosity and sympathy. Locals began showing up to buy the remaining soggy baked goods and donate directly to the park project, expressing support and appreciation for the team's efforts.

In the aftermath of the bake sale, the team gathered to reflect and laugh about the day's events. While it didn't go as planned, the fiasco brought the community closer, sparking a newfound interest in the old park that had sat untouched for years. The incident served as a reminder that even missteps can lead to unexpected support and that their efforts to save the park resonated with the community more deeply than they had realized.

Doris wasn't ready to concede yet and shot back, "Well, I'm glad you can laugh about this, Susan, but what are we supposed to do now? This isn't good at all. Our whole budget was tied up in that grant, and without it, we're dead in the water."

"But think about the community turnout we had that day," Susan reminded her, referring to all who had shown up and even donated afterward.

"I'm sure we can rally the community to help us again. Let's try the bake sale again! Only this time, we'll double and triple check the weather—and make sure the paper has the correct time and date," she concluded with resolve.

Doris burst into laughter. "If we end up with another 'Bake Sale Fiasco,' I might just throw in the towel," she told Susan. "Alright, let's call the team and set up a meeting. We'll need to brainstorm together. A bake sale isn't going to make up for the lost grant, but it's a good start if we want to keep the Belle project alive."

The Society for Preservation members gathered around a large table cluttered with blueprints, historical documents, and coffee cups. The atmosphere was upbeat, reflecting their progress on the Belle project. Doris opened the meeting informally.

"I want to start by saying how proud I am of our work so far. Thanks to everyone's hard work, the Belle is starting to look like the treasure she once was." The group exchanged smiles and nods, a sense of camaraderie filling the room.

"It's been amazing to see the community rally around this project," Susan said. "Everyone I've spoken to is excited and supportive."

"The structural integrity is finally where we need it to be, and with the roof repairs scheduled next, we'll start to see things come together," John added. "Honestly, I didn't want to work on this project at first, but now that I see the potential and what it means for this house, I'm excited to get started!"

The mood in the room shifted as Doris took a deep breath, hesitating before she continued. "This morning, I received a call from the state historical grant committee. Our funding... the grant we were counting on to cover a significant portion of our costs... has been redirected."

A moment of stunned silence followed her announcement.

Helen broke the silence. "Redirected? But how? We met every requirement, every deadline. They assured us the Belle was a priority."

"I know," Doris replied. "It seems the recent wildfires have devastated several counties. The governor declared a state of emergency, and funds are being rerouted to help those communities. I... I don't know how we will fill this financial gap." She paused, looking at each member to gauge their reactions. "But that's why we're here today—to brainstorm ideas."

Frank ran his fingers through his hair, clearly frustrated. "What are we supposed to do now? We have contractors scheduled and materials ordered. Without that grant, we're in the hole." Heads nodded around the room as everyone exchanged bewildered looks.

Susan, ever the optimist, leaned forward to rally the group. "Okay, this is a setback, but it's not the end. We've faced challenges before. There's got to be another way. We can't let this stop us."

"The technical work can't proceed without funding," John added. "We might need to delay the roof repairs, but that puts the interior work at risk, especially with the rainy season coming."

Helen, deep in thought, tapped her pen against her notebook.

"What if we reached out to the community?" Helen suggested. "A fundraising campaign, maybe even a benefit event. We've got several local businesses interested in the project. Maybe they'd be willing to step up, given the circumstances."

"I like that idea," Doris said enthusiastically. "We need to be transparent with the community about our situation. If they see how much we've accomplished and understand what's at stake, they'll help us. The Belle isn't just our project; it's part of the town's soul."

Susan looked around the room, her gaze settling on each member. "We're not going to let this project die. The Belle means too much to us and this community. Let's put our heads together, get creative, and show everyone what we're made of. We've overcome obstacles before, and we'll do it again."

"Ugh…okay," Frank sighed, opening his hands in resignation. "I could try talking to the suppliers and see if there's any wiggle room in payment for the materials we've ordered. Maybe some deferred payment plans until we're back on our feet." He paused. "It's not ideal, and it could backfire… but it's worth a try."

With a newfound determination filling the room, the group began brainstorming and exchanging ideas—everything from community bake sales and crowdfunding campaigns to benefit concerts and sponsorship from local businesses.

"Thank you, everyone," Doris said as the meeting concluded. "I knew I could count on you. Let's get to work and save the Belle. Together, we can do this!" The team's support lifted her spirits.

In the days that followed, their efforts were rewarded with growing support. Frank was able to negotiate a payment plan with the supplier. John found more volunteers eager to join the restoration and even secured essential tools and supplies for the roof. The project was back on track.

With her knack for organization and community engagement, Susan spearheaded the crowdfunding campaign. She crafted a compelling narrative about the Belle, emphasizing its historical significance and potential role in the community's future. Using social media, local newspapers, and community bulletin boards, she appealed to the town's pride and sense of heritage.

By leveraging her connections and the goodwill she had built within the town, Doris reached out to local businesses and affluent residents who had previously expressed interest. Armed with a detailed presentation on the project's vision, its benefits, and the urgent need for funding, she arranged face-to-face meetings to gain their support.

As word of their challenges spread, the community's response was overwhelming. The crowdfunding campaign gained momentum, with donations pouring in—from small personal contributions to more considerable sums from local businesses. Town residents rallied around the project, even organizing fundraising events to support the Belle.

Susan and Doris also hosted a town hall meeting, inviting the community to discuss the project's challenges and brainstorm additional solutions. This meeting became a turning point, fostering a sense of collective responsibility and shared ownership over the Belle's future.

Although losing the grant initially felt daunting, the experience ultimately brought the club and the community closer. It reinforced the importance of the Belle—not just as a building but as a symbol of the community's resilience and unity.

The Theft

One morning, John arrived at the site only to discover that many building materials had been stolen overnight. Expensive copper piping, custom-made to fit the house's historical design, and several antique fixtures donated by local antique dealers were missing. The theft represented a financial setback and a delay in the restoration timeline as they scrambled to replace the unique materials.

Word of the theft quickly spread through the town, stirring whispers of doubt and criticism among some community members. Questions arose about the feasibility of the project and the Society for Preservation's ability to manage such an ambitious endeavor. These murmurs of skepticism began to erode the project's previously broad support, casting a shadow of doubt over the future of the Belle.

Standing with John on the front lawn of the Belle, Doris acknowledged that this rough patch certainly didn't help, especially after their grant loss. But she wasn't ready to throw in the towel. The community had been so supportive, and she felt responsible for them and the project. Her pride wouldn't let her falter.

"It might be the end of the road," John said, sounding defeated as he looked at the broken glass where the thieves had entered.

Doris responded firmly, a newfound confidence in her voice. "The Belle is more than just a building; it symbolizes our community's resilience. We can't let these setbacks define us. We'll figure this one out too!"

John nodded. "Okay, I'm not saying it's time to quit, but this feels wrong. Losing the grant was tough enough, but this," he gestured to the mess, "feels like an insult!"

"I know what you mean," Doris said, her hands on her hips as she looked around. "It feels more like an assault."

"Yes!" John exclaimed, snapping his fingers. "That's exactly it."

As they surveyed the grounds, a few neighbors approached them.

"It's just heartbreaking what happened here," one woman said. Her husband added, "How can we help? Is there any way to prevent this from happening again?"

"We're looking into security measures for the site," John replied. "As for help, any information leading to the recovery of the materials would be invaluable."

"I wish we had something to offer," the man said, shaking his head. "Unfortunately, we weren't here that night, and I'm not sure anyone else saw anything suspicious. But I'll keep my eyes and ears open." He shook John's hand, and he and his wife walked down the block.

As they left, another woman from the neighborhood approached Doris and John.

"Hello, I'm Natalie, from just down the street," she said, pointing to her house past the stop sign. "You know, we've talked about starting a Neighborhood Watch for years, and after what happened here, I think I could finally convince my neighbors to commit. It could save you from needing to hire security on your own."

"Oh, that's wonderful!" Doris exclaimed, hugging Natalie. "That's the spirit we've been looking for in this community! You're a gem, Natalie, and I'm so glad to have you here helping us."

A light returned to John's eyes as he squeezed Natalie's hand. "This is a much-needed breakthrough for us. I appreciate it!"

Natalie smiled back at them, assuring them she'd be in touch as soon as everything was organized.

The next day, Susan—working tirelessly to find help after the funding fell through—was overwhelmed with calls from people all over the community offering condolences and support after the theft. So, when she answered the phone, she wasn't expecting to hear news of a breakthrough in the case. A resident had recognized some of the stolen materials at a construction site in a neighboring town and alerted the authorities. The materials had been recovered, and the culprits were apprehended. The crisis was over!

Doris, John, and Susan stood on the front lawn once more, surrounded by community members, with the recovered materials in the background.

Doris raised her arms to get the crowd's attention. "This… this is the power of community. Not only have we recovered what was lost, but we've also found something much greater—our collective strength."

Everyone nodded in agreement, the sense of community palpable.

Seeing the renewed enthusiasm in the crowd, John continued, "I have to admit, I had my doubts. But seeing what we've accomplished together has renewed my faith. The Belle isn't just a building; it's a testament to what we can achieve as a community."

Cheers and applause erupted from the crowd, celebrating their unity and fortitude.

As the sun set, casting a warm glow over the Belle and its supporters, the project no longer felt like an uphill battle. It felt like a mission that brought the community closer than ever.

After The Belle had been restored, the Club held one more fundraiser to ensure the success and future of the property. It was a ball honoring the grand old times the house once knew. There were beautiful women in gowns of many different styles and colors, and men all dressed in their best tails or suits. The night was an epic success. And as Doris and Susan drank their champagne, linked arm in arm, watching the festivities around them, they couldn't help but feel a profound sense of accomplishment and joy. The laughter, the music, and the clinking of glasses all resonated within the beautifully restored walls of The Belle, bringing it back to life in a way that neither of them had dared to dream when they first embarked on this journey.

"Look at what we've accomplished, Doris. Did you ever imagine we'd get to this point?" Susan asked stars in her eyes.

"Honestly, Susan," "Doris pondered, "There were moments I doubted. But seeing everyone here tonight, celebrating in The Belle… it's more than I could have hoped for. It's like we've given her a second chance at glory."

As they watched, some of the guests approached them individually, offering congratulations and heartfelt thanks for their tireless efforts.

John, joining them with a smile, raised his glass. "To Doris and Susan, the heart and soul of this project. You've shown us all what it means to truly care about our heritage and history."

The Crowd repeated, raising their glasses to them. "To Doris and Susan!" echoed through the room, a chorus of appreciation and admiration.

The night continued with dancing, storytelling, and shared memories of the challenges they had overcome together. The Bake sale story was repeated with laughs and often shared as a favorite.

With its gleaming floors and sparkling chandeliers, Belle stood proudly as a beacon of their collective achievement.

As the evening wound down, Doris and Susan stepped outside to take in the view of The Belle, illuminated against the night sky. The laughter and music from inside spilled out into the cool air, wrapping around them like a warm embrace.

"This is just the beginning, isn't it, Susan? The Belle has so much more to give to this town." Doris said as she took a sip from her glass.

"Yes, it's only the beginning," Susan said. "We've created something lasting that generations will cherish. And to think, it all started with a shared vision and an unbreakable bond of friendship."

They stood momentarily longer, taking it all in before joining their friends and neighbors back inside. Once a forgotten relic, the Belle was a vibrant Community Center, symbolizing what people can achieve together for a common cause.

Milestones

Doris's success with Belle took her through this period of reflection and accomplishment, during which she dedicated herself to smaller preservation projects, each with its unique charm and challenges. This further cemented her role in the community and the Society for Preservation.

Additionally, through Susan's connections, Doris found a new rhythm in life, working part-time as a hospital receptionist. Though not demanding, this role gave her a sense of structure and purpose, filling her days with meaningful interactions and the comforting buzz of hospital life.

One lazy Saturday, late in the afternoon, Doris and Susan were seated at Susan's small, cozy kitchen table. Outside, the setting sun shone through the window, bathing the room in its soft light. A pot of tea steamed between them with a plate of homemade raisin oatmeal cookies.

The pair had gotten together to go over new plans for an exciting project that Frank had discovered: an old skating rink from nineteen-eighty needed some work, and the new owners loved what the club did for the Belle, so they reached out to him. He tossed the idea to Susan; naturally, she was enthusiastic and pitched it to Doris.

As they sipped their tea, Susan gently touched Doris' hand and said:

"I've been thinking about you a lot this week. The first anniversary… it's a hard milestone. How are you holding up?"

Doris signed and looked into her tea. "It's been a mix of emotions. In some moments, I feel like I've made so much progress, especially with The Belle, and starting to work again. Other times, it feels like I'm right back at the beginning, missing Robert terribly. And it seems like it's been forever since he left me, but then I looked at the calendar, and it's only been a year! How can it be that way? I feel like I've lived ten years in this single one." She trailed off, looking at the shadows forming now as the sun made its way behind the trees.

"I understand, dear," Susan offered with an empathetic smile. "It never really goes away, does it? The ache. But it does change and becomes a part of the fabric of who we are. You've done incredible things this year, Doris. Robert would be so proud."

Doris nodded, a tear escaping down her cheek. She quickly wiped it away. "Thank you. Having you here, knowing you've walked this path too, means the world to me. Sometimes, I worry that moving forward means leaving him behind."

Susan reached across the table, taking Doris's hand again. "Moving forward is not about forgetting. It's about carrying them with us in everything we do. Like with The Belle, it's not just a project. It's a testament to your resilience, to your love for Robert, and to the life you shared."

Doris answered with a slight chuckle, "It's funny. Working at the hospital and being involved in the preservation projects has given me something to focus on and a reason to get up in the morning. But it's also opened my eyes to so much more… to a future I hadn't allowed myself to imagine."

"That's the spirit," Susan said with a large grin. You're building something beautiful from your loss. It's okay to find joy again and make new memories. It doesn't diminish what you had with Robert; it honors it."

The two women sat in silence for a moment, the bond of shared experience and understanding between them palpable.

And then Doris broke the silence with a question, "What did you do, you know, to mark the first anniversary? I've been at a loss."

Susan took a sip from her cup and replied, "I planted a tree in my backyard—something living that would grow for years to come. It felt like a way to symbolize the continuing journey. Maybe we could do something similar for Robert? A tree, or perhaps a small garden at The Belle?"

Doris' smile said it all; her heart was full of possibility. "That's a beautiful idea. A garden at The Belle. A place of beauty and reflection. Robert would have loved that."

As the evening wore on, the conversation shifted to plans for the garden, memories shared, and laughter. The sense of loss remained, but so did the feeling of hope and the strength of friendship.

Doris left Susan's home that evening, deeply touched by how much her friend cared for her well-being on the first anniversary of Robert's passing. The thought of spending it alone and seemingly forgotten about had brought sorrow, but now Doris felt a deeper appreciation for her friendship with Susan.

Susan's idea for a memorial gave Doris the purpose of celebrating her life with Robert instead of dwelling on the past and the loss.

Later the next day, while on a lunch break, Doris called Helen to ask if she would help her plan the memorial garden.

Helen suggested contacting the local Eagle Scouts as well. She said she knew of one individual about to get his badge and just needed to complete a Community project. Doris was over the moon with this extra information, and the idea was sealed. She contacted the local chapter of the Boy Scouts and found the young man eager to get started with the memorial.

Amid these new chapters of her life, Doris's decision to invest some of her funds from selling her and Robert's home made a substantial profit in the stock market, guided by Cody. Their professional relationship, built on trust and mutual respect, had borne fruit.

Doris received a call from Cody a few days after she and Joshua, the Eagle Scout, had met to draw up plans for the memorial garden. He greeted her warmly with a "long time no see" quip, and she could tell he was smiling ear to ear over the phone. Cody was excited for her to see her portfolio and invited her to meet him at his office when she could make the time.

A few days after that, Doris was seated across from his desk.

"Doris, it's always a pleasure to see you, "Cody smiled that big cheeky grin, "I have some exciting news about your investments."

A mix of anticipation and curiosity lit up her eyes, and Doris leaned in.

"I've been looking forward to this meeting, Cody. What's the news?"

"Well, thanks to some strategic moves we made with your portfolio, your investments have seen substantial growth over the past year ." Cody paused to type on his keyboard, "Specifically, the tech stocks we chose have outperformed expectations, and the renewable energy funds have also seen impressive gains." Doris listened, a sense of pride and disbelief mingling in her reaction.

"That's incredible, Cody! I never imagined… After what has happened, to hear I, mean, such positive news is… it's overwhelming."

Cody chuckled and pushed a folder across his desk toward her, "It's a testament to your foresight and willingness to trust in the process. Now, regarding the profits, we have a few options. We can reinvest a portion into the market, explore new opportunities, or consider other avenues. Perhaps funding another preservation project or setting up a scholarship in Robert's name?"

Doris pondered the idea of channeling the profits into meaningful causes close to her heart.

"I love the idea of giving back, Cody," She replied, "The preservation projects have become a passion of mine, and honoring Robert's memory with a scholarship… it feels right. But can we explore other options?"

"Absolutely," Cody gestured as he said, " It's your choice, and we can look at other options; what do you have in mind?"

"Well, I wanted to mark this year as something special. A close friend suggested a memorial at The Belle for Robert, and I've contracted with a local Eagle Scout to do the project. This extra money will help make it even more beautiful. I wasn't expecting this money, but I'd like to put some of it into that. And I'd like to reinvest the rest of it for now. Let it grow more, and we can revisit the other option you mentioned; does that sound okay?" She breathed and said, "I've also been considering moving out of my apartment. Now that I'm working and my income is steady, I want something bigger."

Cody nodded in agreement and told Doris he would get the funds out and leave the rest of the details with him: "We'll prepare a detailed plan for new investment options, ensuring continued growth. Your financial security remains our top priority, and these ventures can also contribute to your legacy."

Doris nodded, a smile spreading across her face. She was touched by the possibilities of making a difference while safeguarding her future.

"Thank you, Cody. I couldn't have navigated this without you. Let's make it happen."

Cody clapped his hands together and said, "Consider it done. I'll get started on the proposals. We're not just building a portfolio, Doris; we're building a better future."

The meeting ended with a handshake but was more than a mere formality. It symbolized a fruitful partnership and the promise of continued prosperity and philanthropy.

Doris thought about her life and how much it had changed since she met Cody last year. She was so grateful to God that he caused them to bump into one another. And she whispered a silent prayer of gratitude as she drove home. The radio was playing one of her favorite songs, "Goodness of God," and she sang along with the radio as she made her way to her apartment.

But as she was pulling into her parking spot, she saw several police cars and her neighbor who lived across from her being put into the back of one of the squad cars. She saw his wife standing beside a female officer, her young daughter holding her hand and slightly hidden behind her leg as the officer spoke to her. Doris dealt with their family issues and drama inside their apartment for over a year. The fighting was so loud at times it echoed into her own quiet space and disrupted her solitude and peace. Doris had tried on a few occasions to reach out to the family in hopes of offering a friendship and possibly helping them overcome their issues. They were a young couple, and she couldn't bridge the gap.

Her heart went to the innocent little girl hugging her teddy bear and crying hysterically as the squad car with her father drove off. Doris said another prayer, asking the LORD to guide her as she exited her vehicle and approached Leah, the wife and mother to the little girl, Sarah. Leah was 7 months pregnant with her second child, and she was also crying, but her eyes weren't just stained with tears. She had two large black eyes and a swollen, bloodied lip. Doris wasn't sure what to say or do, so she just asked if Sarah would go with her to her apartment while the police officer finished taking Leah's statement.

Leah gave Doris a grateful nod and told Sarah to go with "Grammy Doris and that she wouldn't be too long and would come get her as soon as possible. As Doris took Sarah's hand, the young girl began to whimper, but then Doris told her she had sugar cookies and milk waiting for them once they got inside, and the little girl began to dance around, excited to try one.
As Doris led Sarah into her apartment, she couldn't help but feel a deep sorrow for the little girl and her mother. Yet, she knew now wasn't the time for tears but for action and comfort.

Doris knelt to the little girl's height with a gentle smile and said, "Sarah, my dear, let's find those cookies, shall we? And how does chocolate milk sound?"

Sarah, still sniffling, nods her head, a glimmer of a smile breaking through her tears at the mention of cookies and chocolate milk.

They moved to the kitchen, where Doris quickly set up a small plate of sugar cookies and poured a glass of milk for the girl. She set it on the table where the evening light began to pour in, creating a warm, inviting space.

"There you go, sweetheart, Doris smiled at the young child, "You enjoy that, and I'll be right here if you need anything, okay?"

Sarah munched on the cookies, her mood visibly brightening in Doris's safe, peaceful apartment. Her little legs swung back and forth under the dining room table.

Once Sarah seemed settled, Doris took a moment to herself, looking out the window at her thoughts with Leah. She reflected on the strength it must take to endure such hardship, especially with a child and another on the way.

When Leah arrived at Doris's apartment to pick up Sarah, Doris opened the door with a warm, albeit sorrowful, smile. Leah looked worn and torn, her eyes reflecting the turmoil of her life. She still had a glimmer of hope, perhaps ignited by the kindness she'd been shown.

Doris said to her with a soft, reassuring tone, "I… I can't imagine what you're going through now, but please know you're not alone. This community, myself included, we're here for you and Sarah … and your unborn child." Leah, tears welling in her eyes again, nodded, her voice barely a whisper.

"Thank you, Doris. It's been so hard. I don't know what I'm going to do."

"You take one day at a time," she offered Leah with a slight squeeze. "And remember, strength isn't always about fighting alone. Sometimes, it's about knowing when to lean on others. If you ever need anything, a meal, someone to talk to, or just a moment of peace, my door is always open."

Leah, visibly moved by Doris's words, managed a small smile.

"Thank you. That means more to me than you know."

As Leah and Sarah prepared to leave, Doris handed her a small note with her phone number.

"I mean it," Doris said, "Any Time, day or night. And Sarah, you remember, Grammy Doris has more cookies and stories whenever you want to visit."

Now clinging to her mother, Sarah waved goodbye to Doris, a sense of comfort found in the kindness of a near stranger.

As Doris watched the pair walk across the hall to their unit, she sent up another prayer for their safety and strength. The encounter, though brief, reminded her of the profound impact compassion and community could have on those in need.

The sunset that evening captured a warm glow and bounced it through her apartment window onto the photo she hung of Robert; it seemed he had given her a sign that he was okay and proud of her growth and accomplishments.

Doris felt a renewed sense of purpose. Beyond the preservation projects and her part-time job, she realized the power of simple acts of kindness and the difference they can make in someone's life.

The Memorial Garden for Robert, situated in the serene grounds of The Belle, was a heartfelt project brought to fruition through the collaboration of Doris and Joshua, a dedicated Eagle Scout. This garden was designed to be a place of reflection and beauty, celebrating Robert's love for nature and his community.

A striking cherry blossom tree stood at the heart of the garden, chosen for its beauty and symbolic representation of life's fragility and renewal. It was surrounded by a circular bench, providing a space for visitors to sit, reflect, and enjoy the tranquility.

- Meandering paths paved with cobblestone wove through the garden, flanked by beds of perennial flowers that would bloom in succession, ensuring year-round color and life. A small, gentle bubbling fountain added a soothing auditory element to the garden, attracting birds and adding to the overall sense of peace. A bronze plaque, mounted on a stone near the entrance, bore Robert's name and a brief inscription celebrating his contributions to the community and his lasting legacy through the preservation efforts.

The dedication ceremony for the Memorial Garden was a poignant event attended by members of the Society for Preservation, community leaders, friends, and family. Doris, with Joshua by her side, led the ceremony.

Doris shared a few words about Robert's impact on her life and the community, highlighting his encouragement for preservation and his belief in strengthening community bonds.

Symbolizing the continuation of life and growth, Doris and Joshua planted the cherry blossom tree together. Attendees were then invited to add a handful of soil, participating in the tree's planting. A moment of silence was observed, allowing those present to reflect on Robert's memory and the garden's beauty created in his honor.

The ceremony closed with a poem about love, loss, and the enduring beauty of memories, read by a close friend of Doris and Robert.

In the wake of Robert's passing, Doris navigated a year of profound introspection. As she traversed the contours of her grief, she couldn't help but ponder the imprint of her existence. Robert had left an indelible mark on the lives of those around him, his legacy a tapestry of impact and inspiration. This contemplation stirred within Doris a poignant curiosity—could she, too, forge a legacy that resonated deeply with others? Could her actions and passions ripple through the community in a way that mirrored the meaningful influence Robert had effortlessly wielded?

The local Boy Scouts chapter organized a pinning ceremony recognizing Joshua's hard work on the Memorial Garden, which served as his Eagle Scout project. Doris was honored with a special invitation, reflecting the bond formed between them during the project.

The ceremony, held in a local community hall, formally recognized Joshua's achievements and contribution to the community through the Memorial Garden project.

Doris was given the opportunity to speak, where she commended Joshua's dedication, leadership, and the significant impact of his project on the community. She highlighted the garden as a lasting tribute to Robert's memory.

Following the ceremony, a reception allowed attendees to celebrate Joshua's achievement. The atmosphere was festive, with decorations that subtly nodded to the themes of the Memorial Garden - renewal and community.

- Doris and Joshua shared a table, joined by members of the Society for Preservation and Joshua's family. The conversation flowed easily, with Doris sharing stories of Robert and the early days of The Belle's restoration and Joshua speaking about his journey to becoming an Eagle Scout.

The reception celebrated Joshua's accomplishment and the beginning of a new chapter in Doris's journey. Through their collaboration on the Memorial Garden, a friendship had formed, rooted in shared values and a commitment to making a difference. In the wake of the reception for Joshua and the blossoming of their newfound friendship, Doris' life had been enriched beyond measure. Her days were now interwoven with a tapestry of new friendships, each a treasure she held dear. These relationships, born from shared experiences and mutual respect, filled her world with abundant joy and connection she could never have envisioned. Doris found herself profoundly grateful for these bonds, recognizing them as invaluable gifts she would cherish forever.

Hamilton

Doris met with Cody a few months after the memorial for Robert. She wanted to find out her options for moving out of her efficiency apartment. She didn't want a huge house but didn't want to rent or share space with others as she had been for the last year and a half. Cody's experience in real estate made finding something else much more accessible. Doris also wanted to check on her portfolio. Recently, Doris and Cody had sat down to discuss her options. Funds were available to help her move into a new house, but Doris preferred to withdraw only part of her earnings at a time. Cody, willing to coach her, offered professional advice on proceeding. Although Doris wanted to use her portfolio to finance another restoration, she was also desperate to leave her current situation.

As Doris walked in, the office was bright and welcoming. She saw Cody sitting at his large desk, already reviewing some documents. Doris entered with a mix of anticipation and uncertainty in her demeanor.

Cody smiled warmly at Doris, "It's great to see you again. I've been looking forward to our meeting. How have you been?"

Doris returned his smile, though visibly a bit anxious. "I've been well, Cody, thank you. I've been thinking a lot about what's next for me. That's why I wanted to meet. I feel like it's time for a change, a fresh start."

"I completely understand," Cody replied, pulling a chair out for Doris. "You've mentioned wanting to move out of your current apartment. Let's talk about what you're envisioning for your new home. What are you looking for?"

"Well, to start," Doris began, "I want something modest, not too big, but my own space. No roommates, no renting. I want a place where I can feel at peace, maybe even have a little garden."

Cody nodded thoughtfully, "That sounds wonderful. I believe we can find something that perfectly suits your needs. Have you thought about how you'd like to finance this move? We could look into using a portion of your portfolio, but I remember you also had ambitions for another restoration project."

"Yes, that's exactly my dilemma," Doris said, shaking her head, "I want to invest in another preservation project, but I also need to prioritize finding a new home. I'm unsure how to balance the two without overextending myself."

Cody reached for some papers and passed them to her. "Well, let's break it down. Your portfolio has been performing well, which gives us some flexibility. We can explore mortgage options that allow you to purchase a new home without liquidating too much of your investment. As for the restoration project, we could set aside a portion of your portfolio's growth for that purpose. It's all about finding the right balance."

Doris signed with relief, "That sounds like a plan, Cody. I trust your judgment. What's our first step?"

Cody leaned back in his black office chair, put his hands behind his head, and began to swivel slightly in it as he thought about what they needed to do. "First, we'll start with the house hunt. I already have a few listings in mind that I think you'll love. Once we secure your new home, we'll assess the remaining funds and decide how much we can dedicate to your next preservation project. How does that sound?"

"It sounds perfect, Cody. Thank you. I feel much better knowing there's a way forward to meet all my needs."

"It's my pleasure, Doris," Cody said, walking Doris to the front door. Let's make this new chapter of yours one to remember."

With the meeting concluded, Doris felt optimistic about the path ahead. Cody's expertise and Doris's clear vision for her future lay the groundwork for a successful transition into her new life.

As Doris drove back to her apartment, the weight of uncertainty had lifted. She felt a surge of confidence and excitement about the prospect of finding her new home and moving on with her life. The memorial for Robert had helped heal her broken heart. With Cody's guidance, she was ready to navigate the delicate balance between her aspirations and her commitment to preserving history, ensuring that her journey ahead would be both fulfilling and sustainable.

It wasn't until later that week that Doris' new confidence and the trajectory of her plans took a sudden turn when, while she was out looking for homes available, she stumbled onto a for sale sign at her local grocery store. Someone had posted the picture of the property on the Community Bulletin Board. The image caught her eye as Doris stood at the counter paying for groceries. She tore one of the trim tabs from the printed page pinned to the board. With only a few tabs missing, Doris felt intrigued and confident that the listing was recent.

A website and phone number were attached to the tiny piece of paper. Doris placed the slip into her purse, and after she returned home and had packed her groceries away, she pulled her laptop off the counter and sat on her bed. The website showed a lush green landscape with ample sunshine and trees in the background. It looked like paradise, she thought. But as she looked through the multiple photos online, she couldn't find an actual house. Puzzled, Doris decided to give the phone number listed a call. The woman on the other end said, 'My family has owned the property for years, but sadly, the old home collapsed, and we had to remove it. The new prospective owner would have to build a new home. But the land itself is worth the expense of building on it".

The website listed it as a nicely wooded homestead with 25 acres and a spectacular, panoramic 20-mile Hill Country view. It boasted peaceful ponds, a meandering creek, and a private well. But it was just a short distance from civilization as it was within 15 minutes of everyday essentials in Hamilton, Texas. The land cost $129,000, and Doris felt torn. That amount was nearly everything in her portfolio, and she knew she needed to leave some funds in her account to allow it to continue growing.

Doris decided to make some dinner and put the thought of buying this property on hold for now. She would pray about it and maybe even talk to Cody about it. While preparing for bed that evening, thoughts of the lush landscape lingered in Doris' mind. The sheer size of the property made her imagination race with possibilities. Reaching for her prayer journal, she began writing her nightly prayers, this time adding a plea for guidance about the land. Doris asked the LORD to reveal His plan for her life, seeking clarity on whether this bold move was right. Her lease was ending soon, and she felt the pressure to make a choice, but the idea of investing in such a large property left her uncertain

All night, her dreams kept taking her to the property for sale. She could see herself riding horses and gardening. There were other women in her dream, too. Most were her age, a few middle-aged. Some had children with them, but she didn't know who they were. And then she saw Leah and Sarah too. They were also riding a horse each. And they had such bright, beautiful smiles on their faces. Suddenly, Doris's phone began to ring, and she was pulled out of her wild dream.

Groggily, she said, 'Hello,' and glanced at her clock. It read 1:34 a.m. Doris, still puzzled, tried to shake off the fog of sleep. Finally, she registered the frantic voice on the other end.

"Doris, it's Leah. I'm sorry; I know it's late, but my water broke, and I can't get a hold of Bobby!" Leah said, sobbing.

Suddenly, Doris was up, her adrenaline pumping, as she threw on a shirt and pulled on a pair of sweatpants.

"Hold on, Leah, I'm coming right over; just be calm…okay?" Doris said that for her own sake more than for Leah's.

When Doris opened her door, Leah was already in the hallway, hanging onto her door handle as a contraction hit. Her other hand was holding Sarah's. Her breathing was labored, and Sarah had tears in her eyes. Doris' heart went out to her.

"Have you tried to call Bobby again ?" she asked Leah as she took Sarah's hand and led her to her apartment.

Leah, trying to maintain composure, said, "Oh, Doris… I don't know where Bobby is. He went to the bar hours ago and hasn't come back. I'm just… I'm really worried. I've tried calling several times. It just goes to voicemail. I don't know what to do!"

Doris took Leah's arm, helping Leah into Doris' unit. "Let's not assume the worst. Maybe his phone died, or he's just lost track of time. How are you feeling, though? Are you in a lot of pain or discomfort?"

"Yeah, a little," Leah gritted, "I think it might be stress, too; I'm just so scared!"

"Okay," Doris said, taking command. "Let's get you to the hospital. Where is your go bag? I will take Sarah to my friend Susan's on the way to the hospital. Is that okay?"

Leah nodded, too breathless to say yes, as another contraction came on.

"We can figure out what to do about Bobby from there," Doris concluded.

Leah told Doris they were to find her hospital bag and accepted Doris' help getting to her car. They headed to the hospital after Doris had dropped Sarah off with Susan. "She'll be fine there," Doris reassured Leah.

A few hours after Leah arrived at labor and delivery, a police officer stepped into her room. Tall and slim, the man was familiar to Leah—one of the officers who often responded to her apartment after Bobby's violent outbursts. Officer Mike Miller wore a grave expression, his uncertainty evident as he assessed the scene. With his duty clear, he approached Leah and Doris. 'Mrs. Lawson?' he asked.

Leah nervously answered, "Yes. Is everything okay, Officer Miller? Is it Bobby?"

Officer Miller solemnly looked at Leah, "I'm sorry to have to tell you this, but your husband was involved in a car accident. It appears he was driving under the influence and went off the road. I'm very sorry, but he didn't survive the crash."

Leah was in shock, tears welling up in her eyes as the gravity of the news sunk in. Doris immediately stepped in to provide comfort. She said a tiny prayer as she stood by Leah's bed, holding her hand as she was trying to weep through her contractions.

"Oh, dear, I'm so, so sorry. I'm here for you, whatever you need," Doris said, her tears choking her. She couldn't imagine this happening now, not tonight, not on the eve of their child's birth!

Leah, overwhelmed by grief and the imminent birth of her child, couldn't respond coherently. The nurse who was monitoring the baby's heart became concerned that the news was too much for Leah and that she might cause them both to go into shock. She immediately called for the doctor, and Doris stepped aside with the Officer, giving Leah privacy.

"Officer, this is so terrible. Is there anything else we need to know right now? Any paperwork or formalities that Leah needs to be aware of?"

Officer Miller replied empathetically, "There will be some things to take care of, but we can handle everything now. The most important thing is for Leah to focus on her health and the baby. We'll contact you in the coming days with any necessary steps."

Doris took the Officer's card and said, "Thank you, Officer. Please let me know if there's anything I can do to help Leah during this time. I want to be there for her."

Officer Miller softly replied, "I'll certainly pass that along. It's good to see such great support like this. Take care of her." With that, Officer Miller left the delivery unit, leaving Doris to try to pick up the pieces. Her heart was heavy with the news, but she resolved to support Leah through this unimaginable loss.

Doris returns to Leah's side, ready to offer Leah presence and support through the labor and the challenging days ahead. The juxtaposition of life and loss was palpable in the room, a poignant reminder of the fragility and strength of human existence. Doris silently vowed to be there for Leah, helping her navigate the grief and the joy of motherhood in the shadow of tragedy.

After eleven hours of intense labor, Leah delivered a baby boy. She named him Bobby Allen, of course, for his father and the middle name of Allen to honor Doris for her kindness towards her.

"Doris, I'm so lost and confused right now," Leah confided to her friend as she held her new baby.

"I know; this isn't easy for you, Sarah, and the baby. But I know God has ya'll in his hands; he has a plan. We have to believe that." Doris paused, "And I just want you to know that I'm not going to leave the three of you alone, struggling to make it through this. You have my full support. I have some friends who would also be happy to help. We will come up with a plan. For now, rest and recover. I will pick up Sarah and bring her back here so she can be with you and meet her baby brother." Doris squeezed Leah's hand and picked up her purse. She made her way to the lobby and then allowed herself to feel the heavy grief that she had been fighting to hold back from Leah.

Once she got to Susan's, her friend had a cup of coffee and a cream cheese bagel waiting for her. But when Susan saw Doris' face, she decided that coffee wouldn't be enough.

"Why don't I take Sarah to see her mom and brother, and you take a nap right here?" Susan offered.

At first, Doris didn't think it was appropriate because she had not introduced Susan to Leah. Susan insisted that Doris wouldn't be any good for them if she were dead on her feet. Besides, she and Sarah had gotten along fine, and they were best buddies now. Sarah agreed, and that was all Doris needed. She gave Susan her keys since Sarah's booster seat was already in her car, and then she lay down on the couch and was asleep in no time.

While she slept, the familiar dream from the previous night crept in. Doris was again riding the same horse, and this time, she saw Leah holding her baby boy with Sarah next to her, and each one was also riding a horse. They were all so happy together; the sorrow of losing Bobby wasn't evident in the dream. It was almost as if Leah had never experienced the loss at all. There were other people there too. But Doris didn't recognize them. Some women rode out in the field, herding the cattle. And others were working in a big beautiful garden. Doris could see a few tiny houses scattered about the property—all different shapes and colors. The dream didn't make sense, but she seemed to be at home in this place, and Leah felt like her family like they had known one another all their lives.

When Doris woke up, it was late evening, and she began worrying about Susan and Sara. She pulled Susan's number up and dialed it, and she was confused when she heard the phone ring from the other room. Susan walked into the living room smiling and handed Doris a cup of coffee and a plate of bacon and eggs.

"How long have you been back?" Doris asked her.

"We stayed at the hospital for maybe two hours, but Sarah was antsy and wanted to play with all the hospital equipment. And Leah needed to rest, so I took her to McDonald's to play and get some energy out. She's asleep on the guest bed now. Susan explained. "How are you doing?" she asked her friend with concern.

"I'm overwhelmed by all of this!" Doris said after a sip of her coffee.

"I'm angry as hell!" She said, choking back tears. Susan put a reassuring arm around Doris and said, "I believe you; I know this isn't going to be easy, or you can just walk away from this situation. You, of all people, know what this poor woman is facing now." Susan paused. "You know that I have this space here. It's not too big, but it's just me here, and I'm open to letting Leah and the kids stay with me while she gets her feet under her."

Doris's face melted at her friend's offer. "Susan…I mean, are you sure?" Doris said as she fought back tears of exhaustion and heartbreak. I didn't think they would need to leave their apartment; I thought, if anything, I'd renew my lease and look after them…." She let the rest of her words fade unspoken.

"No, no, I insist on it; I did mention it to Leah; she's so sweet, isn't she?" Susan said with compassion. "Leah isn't opposed to the idea. Her lease is up in two months, and she told me that Bobby hadn't renewed it. They were also a month behind already on rent. The landlord was generous, letting them stay on because she was pregnant. But now, with her husband gone, Leah will need a soft place to land. You definitely can't invite them into your apartment. The space just isn't feasible. And well, I think that I know you enough to know that you'd be happy with this arrangement." Susan concluded. Doris hugged her friend and said, "Well, it's an answer to prayer, that's for sure!"

The two women sat and talked for a few more minutes, and then Doris headed back to the hospital to check in on Leah before going back to her own home. There would be a lot of planning involved in the next few days to come: a funeral and a baby shower to plan, and Leah getting moved out of her apartment and into Susan's home.

That night, Doris had the same familiar dream. It was so realistic that she felt as if she could just reach out and touch everything she saw. When she woke up the next morning, she made an appointment with Cody. She knew what she had to do. She was going to buy that piece of property in Hamilton.

Two days later, Doris entered Cody's office, and her determination was evident. Cody greeted her with his usual warm smile, though he sensed Doris's visit was about more than just a casual catch-up.

"Doris, it's always good to see you; what's on your mind today?"

I found something," she began. It's a piece of property in Hamilton, Texas. It's beautiful, Cody, with vast landscapes, and it feels like it's calling to me. It's listed for $129,000.

As he reviewed the details, Cody raised an eyebrow, pulling up the listing on his computer.

"It does look like a beautiful piece of land. But Doris, $129,000 is nearly all of your earnings from the stock market and the sale of your home. You'd be making a big move."

"I know, I know," Doris said, rubbing her nose at the bridge, "But there's something about this place. I've been dreaming about it, literally. I can see a future there, a community even. I feel like it's where I'm supposed to be."

Now visibly concerned, Cody said, "Doris, I admire your vision and passion, but we need to think about this practically. You would have very little cushion in your finances. What about your plans for another restoration project? And your day-to-day living expenses?"

Doris waved her hand aside and replied, "I've thought about that, too; believe me, I've thought about all kinds of things. I'd have to quit my job at the hospital, for starters. But oh!" She exclaimed as she clapped her hands, "This land, it's not just a purchase; it's an investment in my future. I can build a small house to start, something within my budget. And as for the restoration projects, this could be my project. The land itself has so much potential. I believe I can make it work."

Cody, Taking a deep breath, replied, "Doris, you've always had a knack for seeing the potential where others see obstacles. If anyone can make this work, it's you. However, I'd be remiss if I didn't express my concerns. If you proceed, you must be very strategic about your finances. We should look into all your options for building on the property and ensure you have a solid plan in place."

"That's exactly why I came to you, Cody. I need your expertise to help me plan this properly. I'm not rushing into this. I want to make sure it's done right. But I also need you to know that this feels right. Deep down, I know it's what I should do."

"Alright," Cody said, holding his hands up in submission. "Let's start by outlining a budget for the property purchase and potential construction costs. We'll also need to consider your living expenses during this transition. If we do this, we will do it carefully and wisely."

Doris Smiled "Thank you, Cody. I knew you'd understand. Let's make this dream a reality."

The meeting concluded with a clear plan of action. Cody remained cautious but found himself inspired by Doris' conviction and vision for her future. They transformed her dream into a practical plan grounded in reality yet ambitious enough to reach for the stars.

As Doris left Cody's office that afternoon, her heart was full of hope. The conversation had confirmed what she already felt in her heart—that the property in Hamilton was her next chapter. With Cody's support, she felt prepared to face the challenges ahead, balancing her dreams with the practicalities of making such a significant change. The path forward wouldn't be easy, but Doris was ready to embrace the journey, guided by her vision for a new beginning and a place to call her own in Hamilton, Texas.

A New Beginning

Doris and Susan started a Go-Fund-Me campaign for Leah. The community rallied around Leah and her family. They raised enough to pay her late rent and give Bobby an adequate memorial. John and Frank helped Leah move into Susan's house, and the women gathered a few weeks later to give Leah a baby shower. There was a tremendous outpouring from the community, but one anonymous gift stood out from all the rest. A five-thousand-dollar check arrived in the mail six weeks after Bobby's accident. And all it said was,

"Dear Mrs. Lawson, I want you to know how deeply sorry I am for your loss. Please use this money in whatever way you see best. I hope it helps you.

You're in my daily prayers,

(Signed) A friend"

Susan and Leah were sitting on the couch, a cup of tea in each of their hands, and the check was laid out on the coffee table in front of them. It was such a large amount of money, and the card was so vague that Leah and Susan couldn't believe it! They kept staring at the cashier's check in disbelief.

"This is incredible!" Susan exclaimed, "But who in the world could have sent it? There's no name, just a friend.'" The mystery of the generous donation added an intriguing element to their conversation.

Leah Looked at the check with awe and confusion and said, "I don't know. It's so generous but also so mysterious. I wish I knew who to thank. Everyone has been so supportive, but this… this is something else. It's a blessing. It could help with so many things for me and the kids."

Just then, Doris walked in and greeted both women warmly. Noticing their expressions and the check in Leah's hand, Doris became curious.

"What's all of this?" She asked them. "You both look like you've seen a ghost."

Leah laughed, "Well, it's not a ghost, but look at this." Leah said as she handed Doris the check. "We received it in the mail this afternoon. An anonymous friend donated five thousand dollars!"

Doris examined the check and card, saying, "Wow, that's amazing! Do you have any idea who it could be from?"

Susan chimed in, "We've been trying to figure it out. The note… It's touching, yet leaves so many questions, especially because the gift came from a cashier's check. Whoever sent it took a lot of pains to keep this a secret."

"It's a beautiful gesture." Doris remarked, "Whoever it is cares greatly about you and your family, Leah. In times like these, it's heartwarming to see such kindness."

"It is," Leah replied, "I just wish I could thank them somehow. This will truly make a difference for us. I'm overwhelmed by the generosity."

"Perhaps the best way to thank them is by using the gift as they intended. To make your life a little easier, to give you and the kids a fresh start." Doris offered.

"Doris is right, Leah. And who knows? Maybe one day, the mystery donors will reveal themselves. Until then, let's be grateful for their kindness," Susan said as she patted Leah on the knee.

Leah nodded, a tear rolling down her cheek. "You're right. Thank you, both of you, for everything. I don't know where we'd be without our friends like you."

Doris placed a comforting hand on Leah's shoulder, sharing a solidarity look with Susan.

"We're all in this together, and you're not alone," she said.

As the conversation wound down, the mood in the room shifted from confusion to gratitude. The mystery of the generous donation remained unsolved, but its impact was deeply felt. Leah, buoyed by the support of her friends and the anonymous benefactor, felt a glimmer of hope for the future. Doris and Susan, proud of their community's rallying support, were reminded of the power of collective kindness and the strength found in unity. The weight of the situation was palpable in the room.

The sound of Bobby crying in the next room broke into their quiet reflection. As Leah got up to check on her infant, she turned to Doris with tears and said, "You were right, Doris, at the hospital. You told me that God would care for me and my kids." With that, Leah left the room to soothe her son.

Doris and Susan beamed as they looked after Leah, leaving the room.

"How about some food?" Susan asked Doris. "I've got some leftover chicken and potatoes in the fridge, and I can whip up a salad with them."

"Sure." Doris replied, "I'm so hungry; I skipped lunch today at work because we had a lot going on….and well, I just now realized my stomach is growling!" She laughed.

"Coming right up, don't you worry; I'll have it on the table in five minutes." Susan laughed, too.

"Then I want to hear more about this ranch you have your eye on."

Leah came out of the spare bedroom with Bobby and a sleepy Sarah. Her hair was matted from sweating while she napped. She rubbed her eyes and blinked, then ran to Doris. "Grammy!" the little girl exclaimed.

"How's my girl?" Doris asked her while giving her a big hug.

Sarah began to tell Doris all about her day. And Doris listened intently as the other women worked on the dinner.

Soon, they were all seated with a nice spread of chicken, potatoes, and a salad with a stack of sliced bread and butter on the side. Susan blessed the meal, and they all took turns passing the food around.

Doris's heart was full as she looked around at this ready-made family. She never thought that she would be so blessed to have such wonderful people in her life.

Susan broke the silence by asking Doris about the property she hoped to buy. She wanted the details, and Doris was happy to oblige.

"So, Doris, this property in Hamilton… tell me more about it. It sounds like a big step." Susan said between bites.

"It is 25 acres of beautiful land, with a creek and a well. It's serene, exactly the kind of place I've dreamt about. But there's no house, just the land. The asking price is $129,000, which is… well, it's a lot."

Susan looked concerned, "That does sound like a dream, Doris, but $129,000 for land with no dwelling? It's a huge investment, especially considering the additional costs of building a home from scratch. Have you thought this through?"

Doris sipped her tea and said, "I have, and I know it sounds impractical. But there's something about this place that feels right. I see potential not just for a home but for a community. I can't shake the feeling that it's where I'm meant to be. But I am working diligently with Cody to figure out if it will be practical for me to buy it."

Leah reenters the conversation, having listened while tending to her children.

"It sounds wonderful, Doris. It's a chance for a fresh start, a new beginning. And… if you're considering it seriously, I'd like to help."

"Help?" Doris said with confusion, "You've been through so much.

I couldn't possibly—"

"No, I insist!" Leah broke in. "That anonymous donation, the $5,000… I want to contribute to the property. It's also a way for me to invest in this fresh start. Maybe the kids and I could be a part of it somehow."

Susan jumped in with surprise, "Leah, that's incredibly generous. But are you sure? It's a big decision. And besides, you are welcome here in my home for as long as you want to stay. I hope you know that."

"I've never been more certain of anything," Leah said, taking Susan's hand. I feel very comfortable here with you and right at home. But this community, what we've built here in the wake of tragedy… I see a future in Doris's dream— a place for healing and growth. I want to be part of making that dream a reality."

Doris was moved to tears. "Leah, your offer leaves me speechless. We could start this journey together, build something meaningful… it feels like destiny."

Susan added, reflecting, "When you put it like that, it does sound like an opportunity too good to pass up. Doris, if you're confident this is the right path, and with Leah's incredible support… well, I'm behind you both 100%."

Doris took a moment to look at her friends, overwhelmed by their support and sense of unity. Then she replied, "Thank you, both of you. With your support, I feel like we can do anything. Let's make this dream a reality together—for ourselves, our community, and the legacy we want to leave behind."

As the three finished dinner and cleared the table, the excitement of planning grew in the room as they discussed the potential of the land in Hamilton. Their bond and commitment to the project solidified the idea of creating something new, healing, and growing together. With renewed hope and a shared vision, Doris, Leah, and Susan began to outline their next steps, each woman playing a pivotal role in the journey ahead.

Cody called Doris a few days after the dinner with bad news. The offer for the Hamilton property had been declined. The sellers were considering a different buyer who had offered 15,000 over the asking price.

Doris was crushed. She felt that this land had her name written all over it. And she called Susan with tears running down her face from the disappointment.

Susan answered on the third ring, "Hey, Doris. How are you today?"

"Hi, Susan. I'm not so good," her voice quivered. I've got bad news. Cody just called me. It seems that another buyer outbid me!" I just can't stop thinking about this property. I know it's mine. I can't come up with a better offer without overextending myself. Our conversation the other night gave me so much hope!"

"Oh, I'm very sorry to hear that," Susan replied empathetically, "It was uplifting for all of us the other night. I can't imagine how hard this news is for you. Leah will be heartbroken, too."

"Yes, I hate to see her disappointed right now, especially with all that Leah has been through. This move onto the property was a big decision for her, and she was hoping for a new beginning, too. I really don't want to tell her," Doris said as she wept.

Susan hesitated before she replied, "Doris, I've been thinking about it. At first, the price and the fact there's no home on the property… did give me pause. It's a lot of money, and so much work must be done."

"I understand those concerns," Doris interrupted, "I have them too. But I also saw this as an opportunity for something significant. It felt even more possible with Leah's contribution, but now it's not."

"Yes, it is," Susan replied with another long pause as she searched her heart for the right words to say. And hearing you both talk about it, the vision you have for the land… It's hard not to get caught up in the excitement. This could really be something special."

"That's exactly how I feel, Susan. But it's no use," Doris said with defeat, "I appreciate your support; it means everything to me. I'm just not sure there is any hope on this one."

Susan paused for a moment. "Doris, that's actually what I've been thinking about. The land, our conversation, Leah's incredible gesture… it's all I've been able to think about. And well, I'm going to sell my home and go in with you on the investment for the property."

Doris was stunned. "Really?" "Wow, that's such a wonderful gesture. Are you sure?"

Susan laughed, "I am, more than ever. I want in. I've been looking for a fresh start, something to reignite my passion, and this… this feels like it could be it!"

Surprised, Doris was beside herself, "I just don't know what to say. We've been through so much together. I'm honored to have you partner with me on this."

"Yes, me too. I want to sell my house and invest in the Hamilton property with you and Leah," Susan told her. I want to build something from the ground up—a new community, a new beginning for all of us."

Doris was overwhelmed with joy. "Susan, that's… that's incredible! I need to call Cody back right away!"

"Yes! Hurry and call him. Let me talk, too. Let's have a conference." Susan suggested.

"I can't believe this," Doris said again, in disbelief. To have you and Leah by my side, making this dream come true… it's more than I ever hoped for."

Susan laughed with excitement, "Then it's settled. Let's do this! Now hurry and dial that number, honey, so we don't lose this opportunity!"

Doris put Susan on hold as she dialed Cody's number. When he answered, she clicked over to Susan and merged the two calls.

"Cody, do we have time to counter the other buyers' offer?" Doris asked, almost out of breath, her anxiety growing.

"I'll see what I can do, Doris," Cody responded. "Why, what's up?"

"Hi Cody, this is Susan. Doris and I have decided to invest in the property together. I want to sell my home and move out there. If we can get the seller to consider our offer and beat the other potential buyers, I'd like you to be my Realtor. How does that sound?"

Cody was shocked and left a pregnant pause that made the two women nervous.

"Okay, Ladies," He began slowly. "I'll try to see if the seller is willing to give your offer another chance. But please don't get your hopes up. If the other buyer has already paid their earnest money, I don't think we should try to counter their bid. I'd hate for this to become a bidder's war."

Both women agreed to defer to Cody's expert advice. Then Doris hung up the connection between both parties, knelt, and prayed. She didn't want to lose this fight, but she gave it to the LORD and felt a peace settle over her. "I'm going to be okay either way with this, no matter how it goes," Doris concluded.

A few days later, Cody called about to burst. "Great news, Doris! " He began, grinning ear to ear. "The earnest check from the other buyer bounced, so the seller decided they would accept your offer. Did you want to change your bid to something higher or leave it at the original asking amount?"

Doris nearly fainted. "No, leave it, Cody!" She said with sudden enthusiasm. I'll let Susan know, but I'm sure she's still set on selling her home anyway. Please tell the sellers for me and cut them the check for the earnest amount. I want this property!" she exclaimed.

"Consider it done," Cody smiled. I'll be in touch soon. Have a good rest of your day." And with that, they both hung up the phone.

Doris knelt down to pray and thanked the LORD for his goodness. Grateful and overcome with joy, she began singing "Way Maker" as she gathered her purse and keys and got in her car. She didn't want to call Susan with the news. She wanted to see both Leah and Susan and tell them they should start packing their things. Their next adventure in life awaited them.

It took five months to close on the Hamilton property. Doris had to wait for her lease to expire, and Susan had to wait for her house to sell. With her profit, they had enough to cover a new tiny home with three modest-sized bedrooms and two bathrooms. It also had a small laundry closet. It was an adjustment for all of them, but it was worth it. And they were happy to be together on their new property. A new chapter had begun.

Safe

Cody called on the women a few weeks after they had moved in. He brought a housewarming gift. "So, how are you settling in with your new roommates?" He asked Doris as she gave him a tour of the land, showing him her plans for the place with enthusiasm.

"Well, Cody," she started, "It is a new adjustment. That's the truth." Doris chuckled. "How so?" Cody pried.

"Remember what I said in your office way back when?" She swept some tall grass away as they walked. "I didn't want roommates, and I wanted more space…." Doris trailed off as they turned around to head back.

"Yes, I sure do remember the words," Cody smiled, "Are you having some regrets now?"

Doris stopped dead in her tracks, almost stunned by the thought. "Oh my, no!" She exclaimed. "No, not at all; in fact, I was just thinking how often we might want something one way….you know, maybe even pray for something to be a certain way. But the LORD has his own idea of how things should work out. I couldn't have ever imagined that this was how things would be. I thought I would be happy with more space and no roommates. Heaven's sake, especially with children. But they are such a joy!" Doris looked at Cody with tears. "You know I never got to experience motherhood. I never dreamed that I would be a grandmother. But this arrangement has allowed me to live a life I never thought I would. It's unconventional, I know. But we are all happy. We've become a family. Sure, there are moments when we three women might be irritated with each other. But it comes with the territory. And we have a lot of space out here to get a breath and some distance if needed."

Cody hadn't expected such an explanation but was happy that Doris and the others were making it work. "So what's the plan now," He asked as they reached his truck. "I'm not sure yet," she replied. "But I know this is supposed to be a community. A place for widows or women in need to come and heal. I have imagined more tiny homes scattered around. And we'd all work the land like a small ranch. There will be cows and horses. A garden right over there," she pointed where a few red flags now stood waving in the slight breeze.

Cody's eyes were big, "Do you know anything about cows or horses, Doris?"

She smiled shyly. "No, not really. Susan and I went on a retreat after Robert passed away. It was a working ranch. Where we got to learn the art of being cowboys," Doris laughed at the memory. "And my father had two horses when I was younger. But since that retreat with Susan, I've not been around livestock in years! I'm sure it's just another adventure, a learning curve. We will all learn together."

Cody opened his door, took one last look around, and said, "Come see me in a few months; let's look at your portfolio. I have a feeling you will need a lot coming in. Ranching is expensive."

Doris said that she would. And with that, Cody drove back to civilization. As she watched him go, Doris said a prayer for his safety and a thankful prayer for her new family and home.

The golden hues of the setting sun filter through the windows of the tiny house, casting a warm glow over the cozy, bustling kitchen. Susan hummed a tune while stirring a pot on the stove, her movements graceful and sure. At the same time, Doris, holding baby Bobby close, sat at the kitchen counter, her face alight with joy as she made funny faces at the baby, eliciting laughter. Leah moved quickly around the small space, folding napkins and placing them on the table with a smile. Outside, the laughter of Sarah playing could be heard, adding to the cheerful atmosphere.

Doting on Bobby, Doris spoke to him in baby talk: "And then Mr. Cody came with a big box wrapped in a bow. Can you imagine that? A gift for our tiny house!" Bobby replied to Doris' delight with more joyful gurgling and a toothless smile.

Susan looked over her shoulder, smiling at Doris' excitement, her face reflecting the moment's happiness.

"Cody seemed genuinely impressed with your plans for the land, Doris."

Doris smiled in response, her voice filled with a sense of accomplishment, "He did, didn't he? I was so nervous to show him around, but once I started talking about our dreams for this place… It all felt right."

Leah had finished setting the table and walked over to Doris, taking her son in her arms. She cuddled him and joined the conversation with a thoughtful look.

"It's amazing, isn't it? How things work out. I mean, Doris, you imagined a community here, a sanctuary for those in need, and now we're starting to see it happen."

Doris nodded, her eyes misty with unshed tears, her memory of the conversation with Cody still fresh.

"Yes, it's like I told Cody: we might not always get what we think we want, but sometimes, we end up with something even better. "This"—she gestures around—"all of this is proof of that."

"And think about the future, cows, horses, and our garden. It's going to be an adventure for sure." Susan said with excitement.

Leah chuckled, shaking her head in amusement.

"An adventure with a steep learning curve! But as long as we're together, we can make anything work.

Susan nodded in agreement, turning off the stove and placing the pot on a trivet on the table.

"Dinner's ready! Let's enjoy this meal and dream about our future ranch".

The three women gather around the table, a sense of unity and purpose binding them together. Their laughter and chatter fill the room, mingling with the soft sounds of the evening as the sun dips below the horizon, signaling the end of another day and the beginning of everything yet to come.

Feeling nostalgic, Doris raised her glass in a toast: "To new beginnings, unexpected joys, and the family we choose. May our tiny house always be filled with love and laughter.""

They all raise their glasses, echoing Doris's sentiment. The moment's warmth enveloped them as they celebrated their shared journey, their bond strengthened by each passing day.

Leah called out to Sarah, playing on the patio, and said, "Dinner is ready! "Come inside, sweetheart."

The door burst open as Sarah, a bundle of energy, ran into the room, her face alight with excitement. In her arms, she cradled what appeared to be a small, black-and-white "baby kitty," its tail hanging over her arm.

Excitedly, Sarah squealed,

"Look, Mommy! I found a baby kitty outside. Can I keep it?"

Sarah approached the table to show off her find. The "kitty" squirmed, revealing its unmistakable skunk features more clearly.

Doris, Susan, and Leah, all in unison, screamed, "A skunk!"

In a panic, Susan pushed back from the table, knocking over her chair. Leah jumped up so quickly that her napkin flew off her lap. Doris tried to stand up but ended up pushing the table away from her, causing dishes and dinner to crash to the floor.

The sudden commotion woke the sleeping Bobby, who, startled by the screams, began to cry loudly, adding to the chaos.

Confused and startled, Sarah cried out, "What's wrong?"

And in her confusion, she dropped the baby skunk, which, equally surprised, scuttled away in a panic, seeking refuge under the couch.

Doris grabbed a napkin to clean up her mess and exclaimed,

"Oh my, we've got to get it out before—!"

Leah interrupted while, trying to calm Baby Bobby, said calmly,

"It's okay, it's okay! Nobody panic. Sarah, honey, that's not a kitty; it's a little skunk."

While Susan rushed to open windows, offered,

"We need to air out, just in case… it decides to… you know."

With realization dawning, Sarah looked mortified at the chaos her "baby kitty" had caused and said softly, "I just wanted to help it…"

Now consoling Sarah while still soothing Bobby, Leah kissed her and said, "It's okay, sweetie. It's a good reminder to check what we're bringing into the house, huh?"

Doris and Susan, now slightly calmer, began laughing at the absurdity of the situation. Leah joined in, the tension easing as Baby Bobby's cries turned into curious gurgles.

"Well, this dinner will certainly be memorable". Doris chuckled with tears in her eyes.

"Next time, let's stick to traditional pets," Susan said through stifles of giggles.

The women worked together to clean up the mess, their laughter and chatter filling the tiny house again, a testament to their resilience and bond in the face of unexpected surprises. They eventually coaxed the baby skunk out of the house with some effort, and they all breathed a sigh of relief. It had been quite the experience. But the sun was down, and it was late, so everyone retired for the night.

The next day, in town, Sarah told Mr. King, the small grocery store owner, about her "kitty." Leah laughed shyly as Sarah recounted the story.

-"And mommy said that my new kitty would need to live outside, but that's okay because she promised me I could have a real kitten of my own." Sarah shared readily. (She knew no strangers).

"Well," Mr King offered, "It just so happens that my cat gave birth to eight kittens a few weeks ago. I'd say it's just about time for them to be adopted. Would you like to come over and pick one out?" He smiled.

Sarah looked at her mother, pleading, "Can we, mommy?" She said with big eyes and hands tucked under her chin like a prayer. Leah looked at her sweet face and knew she had to accept the offer. Doris and Susan had already agreed to the idea.

"Yes, we will take you up on that offer. Thank you very much!"

Mr. King picked up his cell phone and told his wife to expect the pair shortly. Then, the two left the store with their purchases and headed to the

King's residence.

The sun was high and bright, casting a warm glow over the King's house. As Leah and Sarah approached, Mrs. King stood on her patio, a box of mewing kittens at her feet. The scene was serene, filled with the soft sounds of a peaceful afternoon.

"Welcome!" Mrs. King called out cheerfully. "It's so good to meet you both. Please, make yourselves comfortable."

Sarah didn't need a second invitation. Her eyes lit up at the sight of the kittens, and she immediately sat down crisscrossed on the ground next to the box, eager to meet her potential new friend.

Leah smiled at Mrs. King.

"Thank you for having us. This is a kind gesture".

The plump older woman looked at Leah with a warm smile and said,

"Can I offer you some tea?"

"Yes," Leah replied, "That would be nice, thank you. I'm not sure how long we'll be here…" She laughed softly, watching Sarah with a loving gaze as she gently picked up each kitten, whispering to it quietly and thoughtfully.

Sarah had become oblivious to the world around her as She picked up the first kitten, whispering, "Hi there, little one. Are you the one who's going to come home with me?"

As Sarah conversed with each kitten, Leah and Mrs. King exchanged pleasantries, sitting a short distance away on the patio chairs. There was a slight breeze and the subtle scent of honeysuckle. It was a peaceful place to sit, relax, and make new friends.

Mrs. King broke the ice by asking:

"How long have you been living in the area? I know just about everyone here bouts, and yours is a face I don't yet know.

Leah blushed and smiled, watching Sarah,

"It's only been a few weeks. We moved in with Doris and Susan on a ranch we bought together. It's been quite the adventure so far".

The older woman nodded, interested;

"Oh, how wonderful! I am still waiting to meet them. It must be quite the change of pace. It's good to have new faces around here. Please introduce me to them at some point.

Meanwhile, Sarah continued her earnest consultations with the kittens, each interaction filled with gentle strokes and soft giggles as she whispered to another kitten.

"You're very fluffy. Do you like to play outside? I have a big yard now".

As the women sipped their tea, they both couldn't help but smile at Sarah's methodical process, her innocence and earnestness touching.

Leah looked at Mrs. King and said, "She's been talking about getting a kitten since we moved in. It's all she's wanted."

The warm smile from the other woman conveyed an understanding of the special bond children can have with pets.

"It's beautiful to see. Sarah and the kitten will grow up together, learning from each other." Mrs. King replied.

Sarah finally seemed to make a decision, holding two particularly adventurous kittens close to her chest as they both squirmed for their freedom. Her face alighted with joy.

"Mommy, I think these two should come home with us!"

This took Leah aback, and she knelt beside Sarah to meet the chosen kittens. Her heart was full at the sight of her daughter's happiness. "Oh, honey, we only agreed to just one," Leah said gently.

She knew this was a hard life lesson for her daughter.

Mrs. King interrupted by offering her own opinion, "Oh, two is always better than one; they do get lonely. I don't want to pry into your business, of course," she said with a slight grin, "But it's just better to go two by two as the good LORD directed Noah."

"Then we'll take these two," Leah said halfway, defeated and hoping it wouldn't cause issues back home.

"We'll take excellent care of them, won't we?" As she patted Sarah on the head. The two kittens were now close to their escape!

Mrs. King watched them, pleased, her heart warmed by the simple yet profound joy of the moment. "Well, let me get you a box!" She exclaimed,

"I think these two are about to make a break for it." She entered the house and returned with a small box with a lid. Sarah held one of the kittens as it purred, and Leah had the other. They gently placed the animals into the box and set the lid firmly on top.

"You've made a fine choice, Sarah." Mrs. King beamed. "You've helped us by giving these two a good home; I hope we can find homes for the rest."

"Well, thanks again, Mrs. King...." Leah began but was interrupted,

"It's Hattie to you; that's what all my friends call me," the older woman said, hugging Leah. "And if you aren't sure where to worship this Sunday, I'd like to invite you to Littleville Baptist Church. It's a small congregation, but we love new people." Hattie finished.

The sound of Sarah's laughter and soft meows from the box that Leah now held suddenly caused her to weep. She hadn't expected Hattie's profound kindness to make her feel so wanted and loved, like a significant addition to a loving family.

"Oh, Child!" Hattie said as she pulled a handkerchief from her pocket. "Whatever I said, I do apologize. Give me that box before you drop it now, and come back and sit down."

Sarah stopped playing and came to her mother's side with a concerned look. "Mommy cries like this a lot now after my daddy died," she offered with a quivering lip as she took Leah's hand and sat on her lap on the patio furniture.

"Oh dear, I'm so sorry to hear this. May I ask? How long has your husband been gone now? Hattie said with deep empathy.

"Um, I think nine months now; he was killed on the night I gave birth to our son, Bobby," Leah said as she regained her composure. "It seems like it's been longer." She continued, "Little Bobby will be ten months in two weeks. And I had moved in with Susan after the birth. She took me in, and then my neighbor Doris, Susan's longtime friend, had decided to buy the ranch I told you about, and we all three moved in together into a tiny three-bedroom, two-bathroom house. It's just under 1000 square feet," Leah rambled to keep her mind off her sudden outburst in front of her new friend.

Hattie patted her leg compassionately and said, "It's wonderful that you have such caring people in your life. I will certainly pray for all of you as you settle in. And please don't forget my offer of invitation to church. We'd certainly love to welcome all of you."

Leah replied with a small smile. She hadn't been to church since she was a little girl, but she promised to visit and also let her roommates know.

With that, Hattie hugged her two new friends and waved as they drove off with their new pets tucked safely in the box in the seat next to Sarah's booster.

Leah fretted about explaining two kittens to the other two women, but the matter was easily resolved when both Doris and Susan saw the cats and fell madly in love with them.

"Well, two makes sense, if you ask me," Susan said as she snuggled a little black-and-white tuxedo kitten. The other, purring contentedly in Doris's lap, was a mix of gray and brown with some stripes. They couldn't be more different, but they made great companions for each other and Sarah, who beamed with pride at her two choices.

"This one I'm going to call "Skunk," she giggled at her wit, pointing to the tuxedo kitten. Everyone agreed it was a good name.

"Oh yes, wise choice." Doris laughed. "Just what we need, a reminder not to bring more skunks into the house!" She playfully scolded Sarah. Everyone laughed again at the antics from the previous night.

"And this one…." Sarah continued, is Mooshe".

"That's an interesting name," Susan said. Is there something particular about that name you like?"

Leah offered an abridged explanation,

"Her first word was "mooshe", it was her way of saying cow, or rather a female cow."

"Well, Skunk and Mooshe, welcome to the ranch!" Susan said as she patted both kittens on the head. Now we need to get Dinner started, and then we can set up a place for the cats to sleep until they are old enough to go out on their own."

Sarah sat down to play with her new friends as the women began dinner preparations. The breeze from the north had turned cold, and the winds started to pick up as the evening turned dark. Soon, a storm blew through, and the wind was so strong that it sometimes rocked the tiny home as it hit against the siding. The patio swing was being moved on its own and threatened to break the glass of the nearest window.

Doris and Leah quickly took it down and set it inside the door. The rain blew in sideways, and both women were soaked. But they quickly dried up and changed their soggy clothes just in time for Dinner, which was set on the table. The storm outside raged on while the joyful companions sat down, grateful for a dry home.

A very loud clap of thunder caused the group to jump, and Sarah began to moan as she jumped into her mother's lap. Baby Bobby, who was sleeping in the bedroom, also began to cry. Doris got up to care for him as Leah rocked her terrified daughter.

"It's okay, little bug," she cooed to Sarah. It's just the lightning talking to the thunder, which is much louder. We are safe here. For the first time in a very long time, both Leah and Sarah knew this was the truth.

A Place of Refuge

It was a quiet Tuesday morning, and the sun was just peaking over the horizon when Doris' phone rang. Startled out of a deep sleep, Doris reached for the phone on her side table and groggily said, "Hel…hello?" She quickly looked at the clock on her table, which read 5:45 a.m.

"Good morning, ma'am. I'm very sorry to call so early, and if I've woken you up, I apologize." The authoritative female voice over the speaker said, "My name is Deputy Davis. I'm calling because I've been told you might have a place for a young woman to stay for a few days. She's been involved in a domestic dispute, and we don't have room for her at our local women's shelter."

It took Doris a few seconds to register the caller's request, and she began to fumble with her words. She was very groggy from being jolted from a deep sleep.

"I'm, I'm sorry….Deputy Davis, is it? Can you excuse me, please? Let me put you on a brief hold."

Doris laid the phone back on her nightstand and went to the hall, where she saw Leah and baby Bobby on the couch.

She was feeding him, and so Doris gently walked over to her and asked Leah if she could help her with the phone call.

"Sure, let me get Bobby settled here, and I'll be right in," Leah agreed.

Doris returned to her room and turned the light on, but she regretted it instantly as the bright, rude bulb glared out over the ceiling fan, casting shadows around the room. Doris squinted her eyes and decided to switch the lights off again, but she met Leah in the hallway instead. Switching the phone to speaker, she told the Deputy to proceed with the question.

"Yes, I was calling because we were informed that your place is open to receiving needy women." Replied Deputy Davis.

Leah and Doris exchanged dumbfounded looks, their initial shock at the unexpected request evident. They gasped, struggling to find an appropriate response.

"Um, I'm sorry, Deputy," Doris fumbled, "While we plan to one day have such a facility up and running, it's just impossible at the moment. We only have a small, tiny house, and five people live there. I wonder who would have given you this information? We are only in the beginning of planning now," Doris explained reluctantly.

"I apologize again, ma'am; I wasn't aware of this before I called," The Deputy sounded desperate, "I assure you that we at the sheriff's office were informed that you had such a facility for women in need."

Leah whispered something in Doris' ear, and Doris asked the Deputy if she could call her back. She wanted to talk to Susan and Leah first about the situation. Leah had reminded Doris about her statement a few weeks prior that sometimes their plans didn't fit into the LORD's plans and that this situation seemed a divine appointment.

Susan was just waking up when she found the other two women in the small hallway that joined all the rooms. She had a quizzical look about her that was about to be answered, but she said they needed to get their coffee first!

"No good decisions were made before coffee."

As the women sat in their robes, sipping their warm mugs, Leah shared her own experience as a woman who had been touched by domestic violence. She knew firsthand the struggle of not having a safe refuge. Her willingness to sleep on the couch for a few days so that the young woman had a warm place to land was a testament to her empathy and understanding.

"Sarah can sleep on the floor, and Bobby's bed can easily be moved too. It will be tight for sure, but we can manage it."

Susan needed to be more enthusiastic about the idea. They all managed to fit together in the tiny space with minimal effort, but it was an adjustment for her to come from such a large home where she lived alone to this 1000-square-foot home where she now had roommates.

"Of course, if it is only for a few days, I will do my best to make her stay pleasant and comfortable. But I'm afraid this might not be for a few days….I have a feeling ." She trailed off.

Leah told Susan it was a valid point, but these situations usually resolve in a few days.

Doris was still spinning and couldn't believe someone would give false information about their place. They had plans to make the ranch a Community for women in need, but it was still so premature that she hadn't had time to visit Cody about the funds they needed to get started.

In the end, they all agreed to let the young woman stay. But they wanted more details on her and needed to be assured that it would be just for a few days.

The kitchen was now bathed in the soft light of dawn, and the women sat in anticipation as Doris dialed her cell phone to call the Deputy back. Their expressions were a mix of concern and sleepiness. Sarah, newly awakened, joined them, rubbing her eyes. Leah held her arms out to let her daughter climb into her lap.

Doris, on speakerphone, began to speak to Deputy Davis, "We've discussed the situation. We would like to help if we can. Can you tell us more about the young woman?"

"Certainly, ma'am," Deputy Davis sounded relieved, "Her name is Alice Conway. She's in her early twenties, a young African American woman who has found herself in a troubling situation involving domestic violence. Her fiancé was arrested last night. He's not going to make bail and will be charged with narcotics as well.

The women listen intently, their earlier hesitation replaced by a sense of purpose.

Leah said softly to Doris and Susan

"We can make this work. It's only for a few days."

Susan nodded, her earlier reservations giving way to empathy.

"Yes, of course. We'll manage. It's the right thing to do."

Doris unmuted the phone,

"Alright, Deputy Davis. We'll take her in. But we need to make sure it's only for a few days. Her family… you mentioned arrangements?"

"Yes, ma'am," The Deputy confirmed, "Her family is making travel arrangements to get her back home. It shouldn't be more than a few days."

Leah interrupted;

"And Deputy, we'll need assurances about her safety… and ours."

"Understood," The Deputy replied, "We'll provide you with all the necessary information and support. Thank you, ladies. You're doing a wonderful thing."

The women exchanged looks, their decision made, as the call ended.

Susan, clearly more awake now, broke the silence.

"Well, we better prepare this place for our guests. Let's pull together and make her feel welcome!"

"I'll take care of the sleeping arrangements," Leah said. "We'll make it work, just like we always do."

"And I'll reach out to Cody, Doris replied, "Maybe he can expedite our plans for the ranch. This is a clear sign we're on the right path; at least someone out there thinks we are."

As the women sprung into action, rearranging the tiny house with a newfound determination. The early morning's uncertainty was replaced with a collective resolve to provide refuge and support to someone in need.

Later that morning, Alice arrived escorted by Deputy Davis, a tall, slender, middle-aged woman who greeted the three women warmly. Their smiles were also genuine and welcoming. Alice was overwhelmed and visibly shaken but touched by the kindness of strangers.

With her voice breaking slightly, she said to the three women on the patio,

"Thank you. I… I don't know what to say."

Leah offered to take Alice's suitcase,

"You don't need to say anything, Alice. You're safe here. "

Alice nodded, with tears in her eyes, as she stepped into the tiny house, the door closing softly behind her. She was terrified, but as soon as she entered, all her fears melted away. Alice suddenly felt safe and secure when she saw little Sarah and her baby brother Bobby on the couch.

"Are these your kids?" she asked Leah.

"Yes, this is Sarah," Leah introduced her family, "and this is baby Bobby."

"I have some baby kitties; you wanna see 'em'?" Sarah offered.

"O yes, I love cats. Let me see them, please," Alice said with a warm smile for the child. And with that, Sarah took her new friend by the hand and led her to their bedroom. "You get to sleep here in my bed. I share this with my mommy, and my baby brother sleeps there, but we put his bed in the living room. Mommy said I get to have a "camp out" on the floor in the living room."

"O my gosh, I'm sorry I kicked you out of your room," Alice said, turning to Leah.

"It's absolutely fine. We will be okay for a few days, won't we, Sarah?" she asked her daughter quizzically.

"Yes, we will; it will be like a sleepover," Sarah replied.

"Well, let me see your kitties then," Alice said eagerly.

Sarah excitedly brought them out of their hiding place and put them on Alice's lap.

"This is Skunk; she's not really a skunk, but she looks like the one I accidentally brought into the house one day."

Alice looked at Leah and then back at Sarah, saying, "I think you might have to tell me about that."

Leah laughed and told Alice all about the fiasco. It will forever be a fond memory. She was happy she could bring Alice some joy from the telling. When Alice laughed, her smile lit up the room. It was contagious, and soon, all three were laughing so hard that Susan and Doris had to see what was happening.

"What's got you three riled up in here?" Susan asked with a smile.

"I told Alice about our skunk visitor," Leah giggled. Soon, the house was in an uproar. It was a joyful moment to share this memory with a stranger who enjoyed the comedy.

"Lunch will be ready in an hour." Susan finally said with tears in her eyes.

"I'll leave you to rest for now, Alice," Leah offered. "Make yourself at home,"

"And you can babysit my kitties if you want to," Sarah said.

"Of course, I'm happy to watch them for you Sarah," Alice replied with genuine gratitude. Overwhelmed by the emotions of the previous day, she fell on the bed in tears and cried herself to sleep when the door closed.

The tiny house was filled with the aroma of prepared lunch, a comforting blend of spices and warmth. Alice was asleep on the bed, her face peaceful after the earlier emotional release.

Leah approached the door, knocking softly, then opening it just a crack.

"Alice, it's Leah," She said softly, "Lunch is ready when you are."

Alice stirred, blinking her eyes open, momentarily disoriented before the morning's events came flooding back. She sat up, wiping her eyes, and took a deep breath, steadying herself. With her voice still heavy with sleep, Alice managed a small "Thank you. I'll be out in a moment."

Leah smiled gently, nodding, and stepped away, giving Alice a moment to gather herself.

Alice emerged from the room, looking a bit more composed, and was immediately greeted by the sight of the makeshift family gathered for lunch.

The small living area had been transformed into a cozy dining space. Doris and Susan set the table while Sarah and baby Bobby play quietly. The atmosphere was warm and inviting, starkly contrasting the tension and fear that Alice had felt just hours before.

Susan was putting the last dish on the table and genuinely invited Alice over,

"There you are, Alice. Please join us. We've made plenty."

Alice hesitated momentarily before Doris waved her to an open seat next to Leah.

"We're just a big, extended family here. You're part of it now, even if just for a little while," she smiled at her guest.

The simple kindness and acceptance from these virtual strangers brought a small smile to Alice's face, and she took a seat, feeling a bit more at ease.

Leah spoke quietly to her; "We're all here for you, Alice. Don't worry about a thing."

As they began to eat, the conversation flowed gently. Alice listened more than spoke, but Sarah's light chatter and laughter and the comfortable dynamic of the group made her feel more welcomed and less isolated than she had in a long time.

Alice looked over at Leah,

"Thank you for taking me in like this. It means a lot."

"We believe in helping where we can. And you're not alone, Alice. Remember that". Leah said gently.

Lunch continued with more shared stories and gentle laughter. The earlier uproar over the skunk story was now a fond anecdote that brought a hint of joy to Alice's eyes.

As they cleared the table together, Alice pitched in, feeling a part of something. This was a stark reminder of the kindness in the world that still existed, a stark contrast to the fear and uncertainty she felt just the night before.

As the group worked together in the tiny kitchen, a feeling of unity and compassion enveloped the temporary sanctuary, a place of solace and hope for one who had lost so much yet found an unexpected place among strangers.

Doris called Cody and filled him in on the situation, asking if there was anything left in her portfolio she could begin investing in their dream. He told her it was feasible but tight. Cody cautioned her from sinking all her investments into the ranch and said she didn't need to look at financing the money. He also offered that she get with her old friends in Ennis and see if they would help her raise funds as they did for their restoration projects.

Doris discussed it with Susan, and the pair soon consulted Margret Scott and Helen Adams over Zoom.

The women were thrilled to be included in a new venture. They lived for the thrill of fundraising, and Helen had a few connections through her husband, John. The four women put their heads together and began to brainstorm. The Community would need to be included, as this would be a refuge for some residents.

The tiny house's living room was bustling with activity and excitement as Doris and Susan gathered around their small coffee table, now covered in notebooks, pens, and a laptop that held Helen and Margaret.

Doris started the meeting by thanking the women for their time. "As you know, we dream of turning this ranch into a Community for needy women. But to make it a reality, we will need funds."

Susan nodded in agreement, looking at the women on the screen in front of her,

"Cody advised us to be careful with our investments and suggested fundraising as a viable path forward. We thought, who better to help us than the queens of fundraising themselves?"

Margret and Helen each smile, clearly flattered and ready to dive in.

"I'm thrilled to be a part of this." Margret chimed in, "What's our target goal?"

Doris began enlightening the group,

"We're aiming for enough to build a few more tiny homes and a Community center. It's ambitious, but we can do it.

Helen broke in with excitement,

"John has connections with local businesses. We could organize a charity auction. Businesses donate items or services, and all proceeds go to the ranch."

"And what about a Community fair? "Susan asked. We could have stalls, games, and local bands. There would be a small entry fee, and all the profits would go towards our project."

The ideas flowed freely, with each woman contributing her thoughts and suggestions.

"Let's involve the local schools too. Art contests, bake sales… Kids can be great ambassadors for causes like ours." Margaret enlisted.

Doris nodded in agreement,

"These are all fantastic ideas. We need to ensure the Community understands our mission. This ranch isn't just for us; it's a haven for those in need."

Helen interjected,

"Let's also set up a website and a social media campaign. We need to reach as many people as possible in Hamilton and beyond. Ennis is close enough that there could be women from here who must escape to your ranch, too. We need to let the surrounding areas know what we are building."

"We'll need volunteers, a schedule, and a budget for the fair and auction. Let's assign tasks and set our next meeting to finalize the details." Susan practically replied.

The group agreed that each woman played a role that matched her strengths. Margret started drafting a press release while Helen listed potential businesses to contact. Susan sketched a rough timeline for the fair, and Doris took notes, ensuring everything was noticed.

"This is the start of something beautiful, ladies. With your help, we will build a sanctuary that can change lives." Doris finalized the meeting.

Margaret replied by raising her coffee mug towards the screen

"To changing lives and building futures."

The women all agreed, their laughter and chatter filling the tiny house.

"Alright, bye for now, ladies."

Susan waved at the screen, and then Margaret and Helen each waved back as they signed off.

"I'm so excited by this moment," Doris said; the enthusiasm was hard to miss.

"Me too," Susan replied genuinely.

"Let's call Cody. I know I just started investing with him, but there has to be something in my portfolio that might help."

After the productive meeting, the mood in the tiny house was optimistic. With the laptop open, Susan began dialing Cody on a video call. The screen lit up, and Cody's face appeared professional and friendly.

"Good afternoon, Susan." Cody smiled, "How can I help you today?"

Susan returned the smile,

"Hi, Cody. After our meeting today, I wanted to discuss my portfolio. I've only been investing for a few months, but I'm hoping there's been some growth. We're looking into funding options for the ranch project."

Cody nodded, understanding the situation,

"Of course, Susan. Let's take a look at your investments. Given the short time frame, any growth we see will likely be moderate. The market has been relatively stable, which works in our favor."

Cody shared his screen, displaying Susan's portfolio. "Various stocks, bonds, and mutual funds are listed, each with its performance over the last few months." He said as he

pointed to the screen.

"As you can see, your portfolio has experienced some growth. A reasonable return would be from 3% to 5% for someone who started investing recently. It looks like you're right within that ballpark."

Susan leaned in, studying the numbers. The returns were modest but encouraging for such a short investment period.

"That's good to hear," Susan replied. "Do you think there's potential to allocate some of these funds towards our ranch project?"

Cody thought, "It's possible, but we must approach this carefully. Diversification is key in managing risk, especially for a new investor like yourself. If we take funds out, we must ensure your portfolio remains balanced. Plus, we shouldn't overextend. I'd recommend only reallocating a small portion if you decide to proceed."

"I understand," Susan replied. I don't want to make hasty decisions, but there may be a way to support the project without compromising the health of my investments.

"Exactly," Cody replied. "There might be other avenues to explore that don't involve liquidating your assets. For example, interest or dividends earned could be a safer contributing source without touching the principal investment". Cody offered.

"That sounds like a prudent approach. Let's do that." Susan agreed. "How much from the dividends could we consider using for the ranch?"

Cody reviewed the numbers, calculating potential contributions from dividends and interest. And then replied, "Based on your current returns, a modest amount here could help without impacting your investment's growth potential." He said as he pointed to some figures on their shared screen.

Susan was relieved and hopeful, "That's fantastic. I need to contribute without risking my financial future. Thank you, Cody. Can you help me set that up?"

Cody clapped his hands together and said, "Absolutely, Susan. I'll prepare the paperwork and ensure everything's ready for you. We'll proceed cautiously and keep an eye on the market. It's all about finding the right balance."

"Thank you, Cody." Susan said, "I really appreciate your guidance."

They concluded the call with Cody, promising to follow up with detailed plans and actions for Susan's approval. Susan sat back, feeling optimistic about finding a way to contribute to the ranch project while safeguarding her financial future.

Reconnecting Paths

Alice rose early the following day, eager to contribute and show her gratitude to those who had offered her refuge. Surprised to find herself the first one awake at 6:20 a.m., the house enveloped in silence, she decided to freshen up with a quick shower, planning to prepare breakfast for everyone afterward. The warm shower seemed to cleanse her body and the remnants of the previous day's stress, at least temporarily. However, as she cleared the steam from the mirror and caught sight of her reflection, the stark reminders of her ordeal stared back at her—dark circles under her eyes, bruises tinting her lips in shades of purple and red, and a slightly swollen cheek.

The reality of her situation settled heavily upon her, igniting a nauseous churn in her stomach that led her to the sink, gasping for breath.

Meanwhile, Leah had awakened to the shower sound, and sensing Alice's distress, she approached the bathroom door with a gentle knock. "Alice, it's Leah. Are you okay? Can I help you in any way?" she offered through the door.

"I'm okay," Alice replied, though her voice betrayed her struggle.

Leah, respecting her space yet offering unwavering support, responded, "Okay, but I'm here if you need to talk to someone. I've been in your shoes before."

At Leah's words, Alice unlocked the door and invited her in. Moments later, they embraced. Leah provided a shoulder for Alice to cry on, forming a profound bond through shared vulnerability. Their courage to open up and support each other was truly inspiring.

Later, as they sat on the patio, watching Sarah play with her kittens, Leah opened up about her past. She spoke of living in constant uncertainty, never knowing if she and Sarah would be safe from one day to the next. They faced days with little food, and Leah found herself fabricating excuses to borrow money, her ordeal known only to a few close friends. With no family to turn to, Leah and Sarah navigated a precarious existence, always bracing for Bobby's mood swings. On the good days, they breathed easier, but the threat of his anger loomed large, casting a shadow over their lives. Leah recounted her efforts to keep Sarah hidden until she could gauge Bobby's temperament, living in a tense and temporary relief cycle. Bobby's infrequent good moods provided fleeting glimpses of normalcy, making the bad times seem almost surreal by comparison.

In sharing their stories, Alice and Leah discovered solace in their shared experiences, which reminded them of the resilience of companionship and understanding.

Alice found comfort in Leah's presence, and amidst fresh tears, Alice began to share the harrowing journey that led her to their doorstep.

"Hector seemed perfect at first," Alice began, her voice trembling slightly. "We met at the mall where I worked after I moved from Houston. I was trying to start over, away from family turmoil. Hector appeared like a dream, charming and attentive. Before I knew it, we were living together, and he proposed."

Alice recounted the early days of their relationship with a wistful gaze, the memories bittersweet. "I was so in love, feeling like I had everything figured out. But Hector's demeanor shifted drastically. He started accusing me of things I hadn't done, making me doubt my sanity."

The revelation of her wrongful termination from work due to theft accusations—accusations she vehemently denied—was a turning point. "Hector sided with my accusers," Alice said, her confusion and hurt evident. "He convinced me it was my fault, just like he blamed me for imagined financial mistakes."

Moving to Hamilton to live in Hector's grandmother's old shack seemed like a fresh start. "It was a modest place, but it was ours," she said. However, the illusion of peace shattered the night Hector accused her of flirting with his cousin, marking the beginning of physical abuse. "I hid the bruises and continued on, feeling trapped and alone."

"Why didn't you reach out to your parents?" Leah asked, not trying to pry too much.

Alice's voice broke as she detailed how she had left home at seventeen during a dispute with her folks. She was craving independence, and her parents were going through a rough patch in their marriage. The escalation came over her choice of friends and staying out past curfew. She and her father were now estranged. Alice didn't feel confident calling them for help until Hector's eventual arrest, aided by her courageous boss, who intervened and called the authorities. "I was clueless about the narcotics they found with him. My boss stood by me, ensuring I wasn't wrongfully implicated."

As Alice shared her story, Leah listened with empathy, her own experiences resonating with Alice's narrative. "Your strength is admirable," Leah assured her, "Your presence here has been healing for us too."

When Alice's parents arrived that evening to take her home, their gratitude was tangible. Despite offering financial support, the women declined, emphasizing the sanctuary's mission: to be a haven for those in need.

Alice's departure was bittersweet, but her journey at the ranch was a testament to resilience, compassion, and the transformative power of community support. The women of the ranch, with their unwavering support and shared experiences, played a crucial role in Alice's healing journey.

The tiny house's living room was cozy and warm, filled with the soft glow of lamps and the gentle hum of evening. Doris, Susan, and Leah settled on the couch, sipping tea and reflecting on the recent events. At the same time, Sarah played on the floor by Leah's feet with her array of stuffed animals, occasionally chiming in with her own "observations."

"It's amazing, isn't it? How, in just a few days, we've seen so much change. Alice's journey… it's been eye-opening." Doris spoke softly.

Susan nodded, cupping her tea as the warmth enveloped her fingers. "It makes you appreciate the safety and warmth of this little community we're building."

Holding up a stuffed bear, Sarah interjected in her own way.

"You're safe here, Mr. Bear. My mommy and friends make everyone happy!"

Leah smiled at Sarah, her heart full.

"That's right, sweetie. We all look out for each other here."

Turning to the adults, Sarah asked,

"Did we help Alice?"

"Yes, honey," Leah said gently, "We helped her, and she's going to be okay now."

"It's amazing the transformation Alice made so quickly here with us only a few short days." Doris pondered

"Community is all about the healing that can happen when one is given the love and support they need," Susan interjected. "It's a testament to the power of love and support in bringing hope and healing."

Sarah looked up with curiosity.

"What's 'healing'?"

Leah explained tenderly,

"It's when you feel better after being hurt, darling. For example, when you scrape your knee, I put a bandage on it. Remember?"

Sarah nodded with understanding,

"Oh. We gave a bandage to Alice?" She asked inquisitively.

Doris chuckling,

"In a way, yes, Sarah. We gave her a place to feel safe and start to heal her heart."

The women shared a moment of silent agreement, the weight of their mission settling around them like a soft blanket. Sarah, satisfied with the explanation, went back to her play. The simplicity of her world contrasts starkly with the complexities the adults navigate. Yet, in her innocence, she embodied the hope and purity at the heart of their mission.

As the evening wore on, the conversation turned to plans for the future. Still, the image of Sarah playing contentedly on the floor remained a powerful reminder of the innocence and trust they were working to protect and nurture.

Weeks had flown by since Alice's visit, and the fundraising efforts discussed during her stay were in full swing. Susan and Doris, alongside Helen and Margaret, were bustling around the Hamilton Community Center, preparing for the silent auction. Thanks to John's connections, they had managed to secure several high-value items, promising a substantial boost towards funding new tiny homes for the ranch.

One generous company, influenced by John's persuasive efforts, had pledged to construct a barn and corral essential for the ranch's future livestock. Meanwhile, a contribution from the local feed store in Ennis, facilitated by Helen, included a chicken coop complete with a dozen chicks. These additions, temporarily housed in a brooder within the tiny home's cramped living room, had captivated Sarah's heart.

As they arranged the auction tables, a familiar figure entered the room. Tall and slender, dressed in a cowboy hat and black jeans, he was an instantly recognizable presence to Doris. Officer Miller, the same man who had delivered the heart-wrenching news about Leah's husband on the night baby Bobby was born.

Doris greeted him with a mixture of surprise and warmth. "Well, Officer Miller, to what do we owe the pleasure? I doubt you just happened to be in the neighborhood," she said with light humor reaching her eyes.

Removing his hat and running a hand through his hair, Officer Miller, now Mike, shared a shy smile. "I saw your website about the fundraisers and wanted to contribute to your cause," he explained.

Doris's eyes brightened at the mention of their website reaching new supporters. "That's wonderful to hear, Mike. The main event isn't for a few hours yet, but if you're willing, we could always use an extra pair of hands," she offered.

Mike's eyes briefly scanned the room, a hint of disappointment crossing his face when he didn't spot Leah. Susan and Margaret, setting up nearby, caught this exchange and couldn't help but listen in with growing curiosity.

"Leah will be here later with her kids. She's still back at the ranch. Would you like her number so you can get in touch directly?" Doris suggested, empathically sensing Mike's interest.

"That'd be great, ma'am. Thank you," Mike responded, the faintest hint of hope lighting up his features.

Assigned to the heavier tasks, Mike lent his strength and time, his presence a welcome addition to their preparations. The day's work progressed with a new sense of camaraderie, sparked by unexpected connections and shared goals, all woven together by the Community's collective effort to support a cause greater than themselves. After a few hours of help, Mike excused himself, intent on reaching out to Leah with the number Doris had provided.

Leah was standing in the kitchen preparing snacks for Sarah and baby Bobby when her phone rang. She wiped her hands on a towel and glanced at the caller ID. Her eyebrows knitted in surprise when she saw it was an unfamiliar number. Curiosity piqued, she answered.

"Hello?" Leah said tentatively.

"Uh, hi, Leah? It's Mike… Officer Miller, from that night at the hospital. I, um, I hope it's okay I'm calling." Suddenly, Mike thought he was making a mistake, and his voice quivered. But he couldn't hang up now.

Leah's heart skipped a beat at the mention of that night, a mix of emotions crossing her face. But she quickly composed herself, intrigued by his call.

"Oh, hi, Officer Miller. Yes, of course, it's okay. How did you get my number?"

"It's just Mike, please, and Doris gave it to me," he replied. I'm at the Community center right now, actually helping set up for the fundraiser. She mentioned you'd be here later, and, well, I wanted to see how you've been."

Leah paused, a bit annoyed at Doris, and touched at the same time,

"That's thoughtful of you. We're doing alright, thank you. It's been a journey, but we're getting there."

There was a moment of silence as both searched for the right words, the weight of their last encounter hanging between them.

"Well," Mike fumbled, "I've thought a lot about that night. I hope you and the kids are doing okay. I… I'm happy to hear you're getting there."

Leah smiled softly, "Thank you, Mike. That means a lot. It was a tough time, but having the support and my new friends has made a world of difference." There was another awkward but brief pause as Mike searched for the words, pacing up and down the sidewalk as he talked to Leah on the other end.

"I was wondering… if you're comfortable, I'd like to catch up in person. Maybe at the fundraiser later?" Mike asked awkwardly

Leah couldn't hide her surprise, then considering, she paused briefly,

"Yes, I think I'd like that. It'll be good to see a friendly face."

"Great!" Mike said with relief, "I look forward to it. And, uh, Leah?"

"Yes?" she asked curiously.

"Just… um, thank you for being so open to this call. I know it's out of the blue. Mike replied.

Leah chuckled, "Life's full of surprises, Mike. This was a nice one. See you at the fundraiser tonight."

They said their goodbyes, and Leah hung up, thoughtfully. She looked out the window, pondering the unexpected way that people re-enter our lives, sometimes offering a chance for new beginnings or healing old wounds.

Doris's phone rang, and she answered it with her characteristic humor. "Am I in trouble, or is this a thank you call?" she teased.

Leah's laughter came through the line as she recounted her conversation with Mike. "I'm honestly a bit baffled by it all but open to seeing where it might lead," she admitted.

Officer Miller had been a familiar face during some of the darker times in Leah's life, notably during domestic disputes and, most significantly, as the bearer of tragic news about her husband. Until now, Leah had only seen him professionally, never once considering the possibility of any romantic connection. Yet, here he was, reaching out in a completely unexpected way, stirring a mix of curiosity and intrigue within her.

Doris' laughter softened her tone, a blend of jest and sincerity. "It's not exactly a date, not officially anyway. This gives you a chance to concentrate on what really matters to you. And, if by chance this evolves into something more, I'm on standby for babysitting duties," she teased, her chuckle echoing through the phone.

Leah couldn't help but roll her eyes, her voice dripping with playful sarcasm. "Oh, wonderful, you're already picturing me walking down the aisle, right?"

"Life's always ready to throw us a curve ball," Doris mused. "But, who knows? A little extra effort tonight might not hurt," she added, nudging Leah towards dressing up for the evening.

Half-amused and half-exasperated, Leah retorted, "Okay, I'm hanging up now. I'll see y'all a few hours." As she ended the call, Leah exhaled deeply, the notion of venturing into a new relationship weighing heavily on her mind. Considering the myriad responsibilities and emotional complexities she was already navigating, the idea felt almost alien. Yet, Doris' seed of curiosity couldn't be entirely dismissed. The prospect of opening her heart again seemed daunting, yet a sliver of hope flickered somewhere deep inside.

That evening, with the silent auction bustling around them, Officer Mike Miller made his way to Leah, carrying a bouquet of white roses, his gaze filled with hopeful anticipation. He gently asked if she might step outside with him for a conversation. After informing Susan of her whereabouts and instructing Sarah to stay close to "Auntie S," Leah followed Mike into the night. The air outside carried a cool breeze, prompting a slight shiver from Leah. Observing this, Mike offered his jacket, which Leah gratefully accepted along with the roses, her eyes sparkling with curiosity and surprise.

Mike earnestly broke the ice, "Leah, I know this might surprise you, and I hope I'm not overstepping. I've felt a connection with you since that night at the hospital. It's difficult to explain, but it's been on my mind ever since. I wanted to see if, maybe, you felt it too."

Leah held the roses, her eyes reflecting the night's soft light, betraying her surprise and the tumult of emotions Mike's words stirred within her.

She replied softly, with a hint of vulnerability,

"Mike, I... This is unexpected. I won't lie; the thought of moving on, of feeling something for someone again, it's... it's been far from my mind.

Bobby's passing… it's only been a year." She trailed off, the weight of her grief and the uncertainty of new beginnings mixing in her words. Mike listened intently, his expression one of understanding and patience.

"I can't begin to imagine what you've been through, Leah," Mike said gently, "And I wouldn't want to rush you or make you feel like you have to move on from Bobby before you're ready. I just… I felt like I had to share how I felt, but only when you're ready—if you're ever ready, would you consider it?"

Leah looked up at Mike, her heart touched by his sincerity and the respectful distance he gave her. Part of her was absolutely terrified of the idea of starting a new relationship after her experience with Bobby. But as a woman with needs and a longing to be loved, she was touched by the gentleness of the man standing awkwardly in front of her, his hands in his pocket.

"I appreciate your honesty, Mike, and it means a lot that you're thinking of my feelings. I don't know the future or when I'll be ready to explore these feelings. But I'm glad you told me."

Mike nodded, a gentle smile gracing his lips, acknowledging the complex road Leah navigated. "I understand, and I'll be here, Leah. No expectations, no pressure. Just know that I care about you and your kids and want to support you in whatever way you need." Mike held onto the secret confession that he was the one who sent her the five thousand dollars. He felt it was best left unsaid for the time being.

"Thank you, Mike," She replied, "That means more than you know. Let's just take one day at a time."

The next moments felt suspended in time, a shared understanding passing between them. Leah smiled softly, touched by Mike's compassion and the unexpected possibility of new beginnings, however distant they seemed. Mike's heart was beating out of his chest as he looked admiringly at Leah, Her blond hair shining in the moon's light. He wished that he could hold her but did not dare break his promise to give her space.

As they stood together, looking up into the night sky, the crisp air carried mixed emotions and the promise of what could be when the time was right. After a few more extended minutes, Leah made the excuse she needed to check on her kids; they headed back inside. A new layer of their relationship emerged, delicate and unspoken but real and filled with potential.

96

The Gift

A few days post-auction, an unexpected call in the afternoon took Doris by surprise. On the other end was Alphonse, Alice's father. He shared with Doris how Alice had spoken fondly of her time at the ranch and the compassionate care she received. He was informed about their mission to create a sanctuary for women in need like Alice had been.

Alphonse then revealed that he owned a company specializing in tiny houses and expressed his desire to support their cause by donating four new homes to the organization.

Doris was momentarily speechless, the phone nearly slipping from her grasp as she processed the incredible offer. "Hello, Doris…hello?" Alphonse's voice brought her back to reality.

Regaining her composure, Doris responded, "Yes, I'm here, Mr. Conway. I'm just overwhelmed! This is beyond anything we could have hoped for." Her voice conveyed a mixture of shock and immense gratitude.

Alphonse laughed on the other end, saying, "I imagine this is a shock, but I assure you it's a genuine offer. I want to schedule a time we can meet and plan for delivery."

"I'm free anytime you say," Doris said with some excitement mixed with enthusiastic laughter. "Tell me what you need, and we will be ready."

"I'll call you back in a few days. I want to get some things in place and gather my team. We must determine where the homes will be placed and conduct preliminary surveys. I need you to get all the necessary permits for septic and electrical installations done. Here's a website for your county." (He read out the website.) "Do this part, and I'll reach out soon." With that,

Alphonse ended the brief conversation with the promised callback.

Doris called for Susan, who was outside with Leah.

"You won't believe it! You won't believe what I'm going to tell you. I suggest you sit down, Susan," she half commanded her friend.

Bewildered, Susan complied and sat, her eyes wide with expectation.

Leah came in with her children and, reading the expression on Susan's face, "What's happening here?" She asked

Doris replied, "Have a seat, Leah. I'm about to share our best news so far!" Her smile was so bright that the two other women exchanged looks with one another, and then, looking back at Doris, Leah gathered her children on her lap and sat down.

"I just got a call from Alice's father, Mr. Conway. He's expressed his gratitude for our care of his daughter, and that's not all." Doris paused and took a deep breath. "He owns a company that sells tiny homes like ours. He called to tell me that he's donating four brand new homes so that we can get started with our mission of providing care to other women in need."

Susan and Leah sat speechless. They looked at Doris and then at one another.

"I'm absolutely blown away! What an amazing blessing!" Susan broke the silence,

"Yes, it is," Doris replied, shaking her head in disbelief.

With tears in her eyes, Leah couldn't speak but only shook her head as she rocked her son.

A few days passed, and Doris was at the kitchen table with survey papers and her laptop in front of her when her phone rang. The caller ID showed *Mr. Conway *. She quickly answered, anticipation in her voice.

"Mr Conway! What a pleasure to hear from you again." Doris answered cheerfully.

"Hello, Doris." He replied, "I hope I'm not calling at a bad time. I've been coordinating with my team, and we're ready to start planning the setup for the new tiny houses."

Doris's eyes widen in excitement, a smile spreading across her face.

"That's fantastic news! We're all thrilled about your generous donation.

And I've done everything you've asked of me. We have applications with the county for the septic to be brought in. When were you thinking of bringing your crews out?"

"Well, I'd like to send them out and assess the land first to see the best spots for the houses." Alphonse offered, "How does next week sound for a visit?"

"That sounds perfect." She replied, "We'll clear our schedules. This is such an incredible opportunity for us, Mr. Conway."

"Please, call me Alphonse". He said amicably, "And I'm glad to help. Alice told us how much your support meant to her. It's the least we can do. We'll need to prepare the pads for the houses, ensure the ground is level, and the utility hook-ups are in place."

"Understood. We'll start preparing on our end as well. I should have someone from electric company out tomorrow to get the electricity hooked up. Let me know if there's anything specific you need from us before your visit," Doris replied.

"Will do, Doris." He said, "I'll have my foreman, Jeff, give you a call. He'll handle the specifics with you. And meet y'all next week. Expect a call from him soon."

"Thank you, Alphonse." Doris said sincerely, "And thank Jeff in advance for us. We're looking forward to meeting him and getting started on this project. It's going to make such a difference in so many lives."

"I believe so too," Alphonse said genuinely, "I'll see you next week. Take care."

"You as well, Alphonse. Goodbye."

As Doris hung up the phone, a sense of joy and anticipation filled her. She quickly made a note to discuss the upcoming visit with the rest of the team, aware of the significant impact these new homes would have on their mission to provide sanctuary and hope.

"And just think about it," Leah chimed in excitedly at the dinner table as Doris shared the news, "If we hadn't welcomed Alice that day, we wouldn't be looking forward to these four new homes. It's yet another mystery of how things unfold. I'm filled with awe at the way the LORD works day by day, the unexpected yet somehow anticipated twists and turns of life. We would have missed this incredible blessing had we turned her away!" Leah's voice was vibrant with emotion, her heart overflowing with gratitude for the unexpected ways their kindness had been repaid. Her heartfelt words lingered in the air, sparking a thoughtful conversation among the three.

Doris nodded in agreement,

"Leah, you've put it so beautifully. It's as if each step we've taken, guided by kindness, has led us to this moment. These new homes aren't just buildings but symbols of hope and what comes from opening our doors and hearts".

"It really makes you think. How every choice we make sends ripples through our lives. Alice's stay with us was short, but look at its impact—not just on us but on the future residents who will call these tiny houses home." Susan added with a reflective smile.

The three women shared a look of mutual understanding and resolve, their bond strengthened by shared experiences and a shared mission. As they continued their meal, the conversation turned to plans for the future, each idea building on the foundation of kindness and community they had established.

Jeff's crew met with Doris the following week, and they worked together to set up the pad sites for the new homes. A few weeks passed, and the day arrived for the delivery of the four tiny homes. The ranch was a hub of activity and anticipation for Doris, Susan, and Leah. The trio stood together, watching as the first of the tiny homes arrived on a large trailer, the early morning sun casting long shadows across the field that had been prepared for the new structures. Alphonse came in his truck, dressed casually but with a professional air. He stepped out, greeted warmly by the three women. They exchanged handshakes and smiled, the excitement perceptible.

Beaming with gratitude, Doris said, "Alphonse, it's so nice to see you again; thank you for making this happen. We can't begin to express our gratitude."

Alphonse gave a humble nod.

"It's my pleasure, Doris. I know we made the right decision."

The ranch was bustling with energy. Multiple crews worked in coordinated chaos, offloading the homes and beginning the setup process. The sound of power tools and coordinated shouts filled the air. Each tiny house was positioned carefully on its prepared pad, with workers quickly moving to connect utilities and secure each structure to its foundation.

Susan looked at Leah. "It's really happening, isn't it? After all the planning and dreaming". Leah nodded, emotional,

"Yes, it's like watching a dream come to life right before our eyes."

Alphonse asked for a tour of their tiny house and then afterward sat on the couch with Leah, Doris, and Susan across from him. "After seeing your house and hearing what Alice described, I have another offer for you. I know we settled on four homes as a gift, but ladies, I'm in absolute awe at how the five of you live in such a small space." He turned to Leah. "Alice told me you were accommodating in her situation and had a similar story. I'm sorry for the loss of your husband, but I'm also pleased you've been able to get through this difficult time with so much grace and support. So please know this offer I'm about to make is solely based on your friendship with my daughter. And it's not about me feeling sorry for you. It's not a charity. Because I'm offering you your own home for free but with the expectation that you'll let my daughter live with you and your children until she's ready to move on. How does this sound?" He looked at Leah with expectation.

Leah sat next to Alphonse, with her hands in her lap and her eyes on his, but she could not speak. Her mouth was slightly opened, but the words wouldn't come out. Her mind was spinning with the words that she had just heard. "Leah dear," Doris said, "Are you okay?"

Leah looked at Doris, then Susan, bewildered.

She turned back to Alphonse, sitting beside her, and took his hand. "I'm absolutely speechless," she said softly. "Yes, I accept, and I'm happy to have Alice as a roommate; she and I became fast friends, and my children took to her, too."

"Wonderful!" Alphonse clapped his hands. "I've taken the liberty to get the septic and electrical equipment set up, and I just need you to call the company, Leah, and have it delivered in your name. I'm paying for one year's electricity and water for you and my daughter. That will give you two enough time to find the means to take over after my contract expires."

Now, Doris and Susan sat with their mouths open in surprise as Leah began to sob.

"Mr. Conway,"… Susan began but was interrupted.

"Please, it's just Alphonse. We are family here, are we not?"

"Yes, we are!" Doris said as she rose from her place across from Alphonse and walked towards him to give him a hug. "I'm delighted to have you in our family, especially Alice. I look forward to seeing her again."

Feels Like Home

Alice arrived a few weeks later with so much anticipation and energy that the whole gang was in an upheaval of emotions. It was just the kind of family reunion that everyone wanted. Bobby and Sarah were both eager to get their share of attention from Alice. And Sarah couldn't wait to show Alice her room.

"See Alice, this is where your clothes will go, and you can put your bed here..." she went on excitedly.

"Ok, Sarah," Leah said, "Let's let Auntie Alice get settled in while you and I can bake some welcome home cookies for her; how does that sound?" Sarah was reluctant at first; she wanted to show Alice around. But she agreed with her mom and moved slowly to their kitchen, pulling a chair up to the counter to reach it.

"Mama, are we still going to see Grammy Doris and Auntie S anymore?" Leah was confused as she concentrated on the recipe for the cookies.

"Yes, honey, why do you ask?" Sarah thought about her answer and replied, "Because we don't live with them anymore."

"Well, we don't live together in the same place because we have this house now, but we will still see them all the time because we all live on the same property. I bet they would love to taste some of your delicious cookies. Do you want to take them a few once we are finished?" Sarah accepted her mother's offer, and the two were soon whipping up a batch of chocolate chip cookies. Sarah was making a mess, and Leah was trying to clean up steadily behind her daughter. Once the cookies were in the oven and the house began to take on the sweet aroma from the dessert, Leah popped into Alice's room to check on her progress. Alice had only brought a few items with her. And it didn't take her long before she made herself at home.

"How's it going? Is there anything else I can do to help you?" She asked Alice.

"I'm just waiting for my bedroom set to arrive. It doesn't need anything else. Once it gets here, we can try to put it together ourselves. Are you up to the challenge?" Leah nodded and smiled back at Alice,

"This is going to be so wonderful; you'll be like the bonus mom if you're up to the challenge, too," she laughed awkwardly at her words. But Alice also joined in and replied, "I'm looking forward to it, Leah; I've been so giddy for weeks since Dad told me what he had planned for us. Now that it's here, I'm trying not to jump out of my skin from the excitement!"

"Well, Sarah hasn't slept for days after we told her the news," Leah said. "She's been a ball of nerves too, and it's been all I can do to keep her grounded, but I'll admit that I've also struggled to keep my head down here on planet Earth; this is an incredible blessing, and well it's a dream, let's pinch each other and see if one of us wakes up!" The two women began to laugh again. And Sarah walked in to join them.

"Auntie Alice, can I sleep in here with you tonight?" She asked politely. And Alice was all too happy to accommodate her new roommate. "Sure you can, and we can stay up until we can't keep our eyes open anymore and tell all kinds of stories," Sarah began to jump up and down.

The kitchen timer went off, interrupting her celebration, so she raced to the kitchen table, waiting for her mom to pull out the baked goods. Alice wrapped her arms around Sarah as she stayed at the table and said,

"You know what, kid? This already feels like home." Leah smiled as she handed Alice and her daughter a plate of cookies.

"Yes, it does, and welcome home Alice!" The three of them ate their cookies quietly, reflecting on the moment.

Just as they finished eating, the doorbell rang.

"That must be the delivery!" Leah exclaimed. She hurried to the door with Sarah and Alice close behind. The delivery crew efficiently brought in the pieces of the bedroom set, and soon, the room looked complete. Sarah's excitement was infectious as she helped Alice put the finishing touches on the room.

Meanwhile, tiny footsteps could be heard coming from the hallway. Bobby had woken up from his nap, rubbing his eyes and clutching his favorite stuffed animal.

"Mama, cookie?" he asked, sleepy, making everyone smile.

"Of course, Bobby. We saved some just for you," Leah said, picking him up and carrying him to the kitchen. She handed him a cookie, and he happily munched on it, his eyes lighting up with delight.

Later in the afternoon, as the sun began to dip, another knock on the door signaled Doris and Susan's arrival. Leah opened the door to greet them with a warm hug.

"Come in, come in! We were finishing up with Alice's room," she said, leading them inside.

Doris and Susan were thrilled to see the new setup.

"This place looks fantastic; you've done a wonderful job," Doris said, admiring the cozy atmosphere. Susan nodded in agreement, adding,

"And it feels so welcoming. We're so happy for all of you."

Ever the social butterfly, Sarah eagerly showed them around, pointing out every detail she had helped with.

"And this is Alice's new bed! Isn't it pretty?" she exclaimed.

The group settled into the living room, enjoying the warmth and comfort of the home. Sarah brought in a plate of cookies to share, and they chatted and laughed, sharing stories and catching up. Alice felt deeply contented as she looked around at her "family," knowing this was the beginning of many happy memories.

As the sun disappeared into the west, casting a warm glow over the property, Doris and Susan returned to their house just a mile away. The serene walk gave them a moment to reflect on the whirlwind of changes that had taken place since they first arrived. The air was cool and filled with the soft sounds of nature, starkly contrasting the bustling excitement they had just left behind.

Doris felt a deep sense of fulfillment as she considered transforming their once-barren property into a thriving, supportive community.

"It's amazing to see how far we've come," she said, breaking the comfortable silence. "From the initial planning stages to seeing families like Leah's move in and start their new lives. It's all starting to feel very real."

Susan nodded, her thoughts mirroring Doris'. She remembered the countless hours they had spent pouring over blueprints, raising funds, and facing skepticism from those who doubted their vision.

"I know. It's hard to believe it sometimes. But seeing Leah, Alice, Sarah, and Bobby so happy today… it makes all the hard work worth it. They're already making this place their home."

Their steps slowed as they approached their house, and Susan couldn't help but feel excitement and apprehension about the future.

"Our work is only beginning," she said thoughtfully. "The other homes are ready to receive more women in need. It's just a matter of time before our phone rings and someone new joins our family."

Doris sighed softly, a smile playing on her lips as she imagined the new lives they would touch.

"I've been wondering when we will start filling these other homes. Each new person will bring their own stories, struggles, and triumphs. I can't wait to meet them, but I also hope we're ready for the challenges they'll bring."

Susan looked at Doris with a determined expression.

"We've prepared as much as we can. We've built a strong support system, and we have each other. That's the most important thing. Each woman who comes here will find a place to live and a community that cares about them."

As they entered their home, the familiar warmth and comfort of the space enveloped them. Doris headed to the kitchen for tea, a comforting ritual that always helped them unwind after a long day.

"You know, Susan," she said as she filled the kettle, "Today reminded me of why we started this journey. Seeing the joy on Sarah's face, the relief in Leah's eyes… it's all worth it."

Susan leaned against the counter, her heart swelling with gratitude and anticipation. "Absolutely. And we'll continue to do our best, one step at a time. Each new arrival will be a new chapter, and we'll write those stories together."

The two women shared a quiet moment, the weight of their responsibilities balanced by the deep satisfaction of knowing they were making a difference. As they sipped their tea, the house around them seemed to hum with the promise of new beginnings, and they felt ready to face whatever the future held.

Over the Rainbow

It had been raining for three days straight. The ground was saturated with standing water, unable to soak into the soil. The mud was thick and heavy as Alice and Leah did their morning chores around the ranch, caring for the chickens and goats. Their muck boots sloshed and stuck in the mire as they trudged along. It was exhausting work. The women hurried through it as the rain poured down over their raincoats, sometimes streaming into their eyes.

Leah walked with her head down against the wet wind, carrying a bucket of chicken feed. She was ready for the rain to pass. Alice was equally eager to get out of the rain and back into their cozy house.

Inside, Doris was with the children, keeping them occupied while their mother worked. She had breakfast ready, and Sarah was busy with a coloring book, learning her ABCs. Bobby was playing with one of the cats and a piece of string, his laughter infectious. Doris watched him and smiled at his antics.

Suddenly, her cell phone rang. Margaret, her friend from the Preservation Society, called to ask a favor.

"Well, Margaret, how are you?" Doris asked, pleased to hear from her friend, as they hadn't spoken in a while.

"Oh, I'm well enough. I wanted to ask you and Susan a favor, though. Feel free to give it some thought. And I understand it's not one I expect you to make quickly. You see, my Aunt Tally just lost her husband, my Uncle Fred. He left her absolutely destitute!" Margaret sighed. "It breaks my heart, but she's got nothing except the clothes on her back."

"Well, she's welcome here, no question about it," Doris replied.

"There is more to it; I want you and Susan to consider this. You see, Aunt

Tally has early-onset dementia."

"Oh my, I see what you're saying, Margaret," Doris said with reluctance.

"Yes." Margaret continued, "For now, she can do most things independently. It's her anxiety that causes her issues. Understandably so. When she's confused, she gets anxious and needs someone to encourage her. I don't want to see her go into a home, not just yet." She concluded with empathy.

"Let Susan and I discuss this with the other two women. Since Susan was a nurse and from my own work at the hospital, she and I have some experience with people with memory care needs. But I do not know how the other two might feel; having to care for someone's mental health might concern them. I'll call you back later if that's okay," Doris concluded.

"Yes, take some time, and I appreciate it very much," Margaret said with gratitude.

Doris waited for Leah and Alice to return from their chores and clean up before she called a meeting. Susan came over, and Doris explained Margaret's call while watching the emotions play out across the faces of her companions.

They deliberated the situation, carefully considering its implications at the kitchen table; the gravity of the decision hung in the air, mingling with the faint aroma of breakfast and the sound of rain tapping against the windows.

Leah was the first to speak, her voice tinged with concern.

"I can't imagine what it's like for her. Losing her husband and dealing with dementia on top of it. It's heartbreaking. But how much extra care are we supposed to give her? It's not just the physical care, but the emotional strain that worries me."

Alice nodded, her expression thoughtful.

"We have to be realistic about what we can handle. Caring for someone with dementia isn't easy, and we already have so much on our plates with the ranch and the kids."

Susan, always the pragmatic one, leaned forward, her eyes severe.

"We've handled other difficult situations before, but I appreciate that this is different. It's a long-term commitment that could be very challenging. We must consider how it will affect us all."

Doris sighed, feeling the burden of the decision.

"I know it's a lot to ask. But Tally has no one else. And if we don't help her, she might end up in a home, which could make her condition worse. We must weigh our ability to help against the potential impact on our lives." Her words conveyed the sense of responsibility everyone else felt, the weight of their decision evident.

Leah spoke up again, her tone softer.

"It's not just about the practical side, though. There's an emotional aspect, too. We'd be taking in someone vulnerable and scared. I know we'd be allowing her to feel safe and loved. I think that's something worth considering. But my fear is that she's too vulnerable. I also do not want my children harmed if something might get out of hand."

Alice looked at each of them in turn, her expression a mix of resolve and hesitation.

"I agree with Leah. We need to be honest about our limits. We must ensure we're not putting ourselves in a situation we can't handle."

Susan nodded, her eyes thoughtful.

"Perhaps we can take it one step at a time. Maybe start by having Tally visit for a short while and see how she adjusts and how we manage. If it becomes too much, we can look for other options."

Doris felt a surge of gratitude for her friends' understanding and support.

"That sounds like a reasonable plan. I'll call Margaret back and let her know we're willing to try it for a few days at first."

As they reached a tentative decision, a sense of relief and apprehension settled over the group. They were committed to facing this new challenge together, supporting each other and Tally as best they could. But the younger women doubted their ability to care for Tally. They needed to gain the experience and skills to manage someone with memory care needs.

Tally arrived a few days later. Her eyes were dull from grief and fear of the unknown. Doris, being the leader, extended her a warm, welcoming hug, which Tally returned with gratitude.

"Well, I'm here, somewhere over the rainbow, it seems," Tally said with a small smile. "I knew I would live far away, but I didn't think I'd be almost to OZ!"

Everyone laughed awkwardly, unsure if Tally was joking or serious. Because of her dementia, they didn't know which Tally they were meeting—the lucid one or the one who was only slightly aware of her situation.

Susan and Doris set to get Tally settled into Leah's old room. They fluffed the pillows, arranged fresh flowers on the nightstand, and ensured everything was comfortable and inviting. Margaret hovered nearby, her eyes darting between her Aunt and the women, clearly anxious about how her Aunt would adjust.

After Tally was comfortably situated, Margaret and Doris stepped outside momentarily, finding a quiet spot on the porch where they could talk without being overheard.

"How is she really doing, Margaret?" Doris asked gently, her eyes filled with concern.

Margaret sighed, looking out at the rain-soaked landscape.

"Most days, she's very confused. There are moments when she's aware of what's happening, but they're becoming fewer and farther between. She knows she's moving to the ranch on a trial visit, but I'm unsure how much she truly understands."

Doris nodded, her heart aching for both Tally and Margaret. "It must be so hard for her and for you too."

Margaret's eyes glistened with un-shed tears.

"It is. She was always so independent, so full of life. Watching her fade like this is devastating. But I didn't want to put her in a home. I couldn't do that to her, not yet."

Doris reached out, placing a comforting hand on Margaret's arm.

"We'll do our best to help her feel at home here. We'll take it one day at a time and see how she adjusts. And if it becomes too much, we'll find another solution together."

Margaret smiled gratefully.

"Thank you, Doris. Knowing she's with caring people makes this a little easier. I hope she can find some peace here."

"We'll make sure she does," Doris assured her. "We're in this together and will do everything we can to make her feel safe and loved."

Back inside, Susan was giving Tally a gentle tour of the house.

"This is the kitchen, where we'll prepare meals together. And over here is the living room, a perfect spot for reading or relaxing."

Tally looked around, her expression a mixture of curiosity and confusion.

"It's very nice. I'm sorry if I'm a bother."

"You're not a bother at all," Susan said warmly. "We're happy to have you here. Take your time to get used to everything."

Margaret and Doris rejoined them, and Margaret took Tally's hand. "Aunt Tally, you're in good hands. These wonderful women will care for you, and I'll visit often."

Tally's eyes softened, a brief flicker of understanding and gratitude passing through them.

"Thank you, Margaret. I'll try to remember that."

Susan took Tally outside to continue the tour, showing her the ranch's ins and outs.

Doris felt a deep sense of purpose. They had taken on a difficult challenge but were committed to making it work. Together, they would create a new home for Tally filled with care, support, and love.

The next day that followed Tally's arrival was a whirlwind of adjustment and discovery. The women consciously tried to integrate Tally into their daily routine, offering her small tasks that gave her a sense of purpose without overwhelming her.

Leah dropped her children off at Susan and Doris' place as it continued to rain.

Doris asked Tally if she could watch the kids while Leah and Alice did their chores.

Sitting at the kitchen table with Sarah and Bobby, Doris found Tally engaging and vigilant. The children had taken to Tally almost immediately, sensing her vulnerability and responding with the boundless compassion that only children possess.

"Grandma Tally, can you help me with my coloring?" Sarah asked, sliding her coloring book over.

Tally smiled, a genuine warmth in her eyes. "Of course, sweetheart. Let's make this butterfly as colorful as we can."

Not wanting to be left out, Bobby brought over his toy cars. " Vroom vroom!" He made the sound for his cars.

Tally laughed, and the sound was light and joyful. "Oh, Bobby, that's the fastest car I've ever seen!"

As Doris watched, she saw the positive effect the children were having on Tally. Moments of clarity and joy seemed to brighten her day. She made a mental note to encourage more interactions like this.

That afternoon, Tally joined Alice and Leah outside, under the porch's protection, watching the rain and chatting about life on the ranch. Concerned about the impact on her children, Leah was pleasantly surprised by how naturally Tally fit into their lives.

In the evening, Doris and Susan sat with Tally in their living room, sipping tea and talking quietly.

"Tally, how are you finding everything?" Doris asked gently.

Tally looked around, her eyes thoughtful. "It's lovely here. I feel…safe. Sarah and Bobby are delightful, too. They help me to have some clarity."

Susan smiled, relieved. "I am glad to hear that," she remarked.

The next day, the rain stopped, leaving the ranch glistening under a bright, clear sky. Tally joined the women and children outside as they resumed their chores, and her presence was a comforting addition to the team.

As Sarah and Bobby ran around, laughing and playing, Tally watched them serenely. She picked up a small rake and started helping to clear away some of the debris left by the storm.

"Careful, Grandma Tally," Sarah called out. "You don't want to get stuck in the mud!"

Tally chuckled, enjoying the light-heartedness of the moment. "I'll be careful, honey, don't you worry."

Later that afternoon, Doris found Tally sitting on a bench, watching the chickens peck around in the yard. She sat down beside her, grateful for a moment to rest.

"You seem to be settling in well," Doris observed.

Tally nodded, her gaze still on the chickens.

"Yes, I think I am. You know, I grew up on a ranch." She paused, her expression softening with a distant look.

"I didn't know that," Doris replied thoughtfully.

"Yes," Tally continued, "My daddy had a few acres, and I helped my mama with the garden and the chickens. It's been a long time since I felt this... connected. Thank you for giving me a home. I know I'll be okay here."

Doris squeezed Tally's hand. "You're welcome. We're happy to have you here, too."

As the sun set over the ranch, painting the horizon in shades of orange and pink, the women gathered on the porch, savoring the stillness of the evening. Tally sat among them, a sense of peace and belonging settling over her like a warm blanket.

When Susan asked if she'd like to care for the chickens, Tally's eyes lit up with excitement.

"I'd love to," she said, her voice brimming with joy.

Later that night, as Tally lay in her room, she hummed a familiar tune her mother used to sing to her. For the first time in years, she felt truly at home.

Some Kind of Ship

The days began to run together, a whirlwind of activity that kept the group busy with chores and endless projects on the ranch.

As the women worked tirelessly in the garden, Tally cared for the chickens and goats. Having grown up on a farm, she showed a great aptitude for this activity. Susan's suggestion that Tally take over these tasks freed Alice and Leah to help with other pressing projects on the ranch.

One hot, blistering morning, the four women started working on the fences they had begun to build for the additional animals they planned to receive soon. The ranch was slowly taking shape, and the vision became more real daily.

Despite the hard work, camaraderie and shared purpose kept them going. Sarah and Bobby played alongside Tally as she fed the chickens and gave the goats water, chatting with them about when she was a girl, helping her own mother care for the animals. Sarah hung on her every word. She loved the animals on their farm, and she liked helping Grandma Tally corral the chickens and collect the eggs. But soon, her enthusiasm with the animals waned, and Sarah took her brother Bobby by the hand, and they raced around the ranch chasing butterflies and grasshoppers, sometimes getting in the way as the other four women worked to pull some of the fence tighter. Their laughter and innocent mischief brought a lightness to the laborious tasks, even as it sometimes added to the chaos.

As the sun beat down relentlessly, and the heat was oppressive, sweat dripped from their brows and made their muscles ache from the unaccustomed exertion. The atmosphere was tense, and tempers were beginning to fray.

"I think we need to face it and hire a professional here to help us," Susan said with some frustration as they struggled with a roll of hogwire.

"We have to learn to handle this, Susan," Doris quipped back, her tone resolute. "We have to be self-sufficient. Besides, we learned how to do this on that dude ranch we stayed at!"

Her patience wore thin; Susan said, "Yes, but we had some help, too. The guys were there to offer guidance and muscle! I'm soaked with sweat and sore all over. We've been at this for days and haven't been able to finish a row! All I'm saying is let's be realistic here. This will take too much time, even with the four of us together. I don't want to work on this anymore!"

With that, Susan threw down her work gloves, wiped the moisture off her face with her sleeve, and walked back to the house.

Leah and Alice looked on in shock at Susan's sudden outburst. Ever the peaceful and pragmatic one, this was a side they hadn't ever seen. The tension in the air was intense, and the atmosphere shifted from hopeful to strained instantly.

"Let's take a break; get some lemonade and rest for a while. I'll talk to Susan," Doris said, her voice soothing but firm. She followed her friend back to their house, leaving Leah and Alice to gather their thoughts.

In the cool shade of the patio, Doris found Susan sitting with her head in her hands, tears of frustration streaming down her cheeks.

"Susan," Doris said softly, sitting down next to her. "It's okay to feel overwhelmed. This is hard work, and you are right; it's not something we can do alone."

Susan looked up, her eyes red and puffy. "I just feel like we're failing, Doris. We had big dreams for this place, and now it feels like we're sinking."

Doris comforted her friend, saying, "We're not failing. We're just hitting a rough patch. We must remember why we started this and take it one step at a time. Maybe we need extra hands, and there's no shame in that."

Just then, the sound of a car pulling up the driveway caught their attention. Doris looked up to see Officer Miller stepping out of his patrol car. He walked over with a friendly wave. "Afternoon, ladies. I was in the neighborhood and thought I'd stop by to see how things are going."

"Just in the neighborhood, you say?" Doris and Susan exchanged a knowing glance with one another.

Leah and Alice joined Doris and Susan, and Leah's heart skipped a beat when she saw Mike on the patio. He immediately caught Leah's eye. He walked down the steps with a friendly wave, his uniform crisp and his demeanor calm. The sun glinted off his badge, adding a touch of formality to his unexpected visit. She quickly filled Mike in on their struggles with the fencing.

"It's been a bit more than we can handle," she admitted, feeling relief and embarrassment.

Mike nodded thoughtfully. "Fencing is tough work. How about I round up a few of my work companions to give you a hand? We can come by this weekend and finish it in no time."

The offer was a lifeline, and Doris felt a surge of gratitude. "That would be amazing. Thank you so much."

Susan managed a small smile through her tears. "Thank you. We could really use the help."

Mike smiled warmly. "It's no problem at all. I want to be of help. Now, why don't you take a break and get some rest? We'll be here first thing Saturday morning."

As he said this, he looked at Leah with a boyish grin. The other three women smiled secretly at each other, and the tension dissipated. The promise of help brought a renewed sense of hope and determination.

"Well, have a seat, Officer Miller, and I'll pour you a glass of lemonade." Doris offered, giving up her seat to Mike, as she went inside to get another glass. As he waited, Mike turned to Leah and asked, "How have you been, Leah? I've been thinking about you."

Leah felt the heat rise to her face and struggled to find her voice. "Oh, you know, just busy with the ranch and all," she said, her words tumbling out awkwardly. She shifted her weight from one foot to the other, acutely aware of the other's attention.

Still looking at Leah with that charming grin, he said, "I'm glad you're doing well. It's a beautiful place you've got here." Leah nodded, her heart pounding.

"Thanks," she blushed.

Susan, sensing Leah's discomfort, stepped in smoothly. "Why don't you two take a walk? Then you can look at the fence and our progress," she offered.

Leah set her glass down and smiled at her friend for the suggestion as she turned to go down the steps,

"Shall we?" She gestured to Mike to follow towards the fence. Mike sheepishly took his cue and willingly excused himself, letting Leah lead the way. Doris returned with a glass of lemonade and sat back in her seat. "Well, I, for one, am happy to see these two together. Whatever comes of it, they sure make a handsome couple." Susan and Alice agreed as they sipped their beverages, as the afternoon heat and recent arguments were cooling.

Mike and Leah walked the fence line together in awkward silence before Mike cleared his throat. "Um, Leah, are we okay?" he asked timidly.

Leah stopped walking and turned to face Mike. She was full of nervous energy and processing a million thoughts through her exhausted mind.

"Yes, I think so. Why do you ask like that, Mike?" She looked at him with genuine interest.

Mike shoved his hands in his pocket and kicked a rock.

"Well, you haven't returned my text messages for weeks now, and I wasn't sure what had changed between us."

For a split second, Leah felt a tinge of annoyance toward Mike. She had been clear about needing time to think over their relationship, and his sudden unannounced visit had her feeling a mixture of emotions.

"I've honestly just been busy with the ranch and my kids; I'm sorry that I haven't returned your messages and left you hanging. But you also agreed to give me time to think." She ended briskly.

"Hey!" "I'm sorry, Leah," Mike said, reaching for her hand. He gently took it in his, and they began to walk again. Leah melted at his touch, her heart beating faster now. "I was hoping we could talk now. If you're open to it," Mike said.

Leah sighed, looking at the ground as they walked. "I don't know, Mike.

It's just been so overwhelming. Losing Bobby… and now, thinking about what's next for me, for my kids. It's all so much. And it's not that I haven't given us more thought. I really haven't had the time to focus on the idea of starting something new."

Mike squeezed her hand reassuringly. "I get that. I really do. I don't want to rush you or make you feel pressured. I just want to be here for you, however you need me."

Leah stopped again, taking a deep breath before meeting Mike's eyes. "I appreciate that, truly. It's just that I'm not sure I'm ready for anything more than friendship right now. I need more time to figure things out."

Mike nodded, his expression soft and understanding. "That's okay, Leah. I can wait. I care about you, and I'll be here when you're ready, even if it's just as a friend."

Leah felt a wave of relief wash over her. "Thank you, Mike. That means a lot to me. I need to take things one step at a time, and helping Doris and Susan with this project is a lot of work. You showed up just in the nick of time today! "

"Oh yeah, you mean I'm actually the hero?" Mike teased back.

"Well, sort of," Leah blushed, "Susan and Doris argued over the fence just before you showed up. We really do have our work cut out for us. And Susan is right; we are way over our heads. Thank you for offering to help this weekend."

They continued walking in silence, the tension easing between them. And then Mike spoke again, and Leah looked towards him as he said: "I'm here for you; please don't forget that, no matter what." And with that, he lifted her hand to his lips and gently kissed it. Leah's breath was caught in her throat at his gesture, and she felt like she should just let him kiss her; she stopped and stared at his face, his eyes burning with desire, staring back at hers. But he took a step backward and adjusted his utility belt. "I need to get back to Ennis; I was in the neighborhood helping the Hamilton department with a burglary case. But I have to get back to my own jurisdiction now."

"Okay, I'm glad you came by, and we all will be happy to see you this weekend," Leah said as they returned to the house.

Mike waved to the others as he got back in his squad car. Promising to return with plenty of help. And with that, he drove off, leaving some dust in the air. Leah waved the dust away from her face and saw her friends staring at her. They weren't trying to hide their amusement. Looking back at her with inquisitive eyes.

Leah laughed and said, "Oh, stop! We are just friends."

But Alice didn't buy it. "Uh-oh, I believe we have a case of denial!"

"No, I'm serious, though!" Leah shot back, annoyed. "I've told him we are just friends."

"Girl, please!" Alice said, "You might not know what kind of ship you are in, but I guarantee it's not a friendship." Leah rolled her eyes and grabbed her gloves as Susan and Doris watched and listened silently, reflecting on the situation.

"I'm going to work in the garden if anyone feels like joining," Leah said hotly as she walked away.

"It's okay, Alice," Doris interjected, "Leah has much to consider when getting into another romantic relationship. She's not upset at you or any of us. She's just confused, and I think she likes Officer Miller; she's just scared to admit it."

Leah's mind was a whirlwind as she knelt in the garden, her fingers working through the soil with practiced ease. The rhythmic motions of planting and weeding brought her a semblance of peace, but her mind was anything but calm. Leah repeatedly replayed her conversation with Mike, analyzing every word, look, and touch.

She knew Mike's patience and understanding were genuine, but she couldn't shake the guilt of keeping him in limbo. The guilt mingled with a deep-seated fear—fear of moving on too quickly, fear of betraying Bobby's memory, and fear of opening herself up to the vulnerability of loving someone again. Her heart was a battlefield, torn between the past Leah cherished and the future she was too scared to embrace.

Tally had been in the garden when Leah arrived, and she could discern that Leah was upset. But she wasn't sure why.

"That gentleman of yours is surely a handsome one. I remember when my

Fred was courting me. He was a gentleman, too. It took me a while to let him take me around. I was too nervous about what others would say. But eventually, he won me over. I'm going to miss him! Don't you let love go stale, honey! You just never know how long you have." Tally advised as she pulled weeds next to Leah.

As Leah dug out weeds and planted new flowers, Leah listened to Tally reminisce about her childhood and her younger married life with Fred. The sun began to dip below the horizon, casting a warm golden glow over the garden, and Leah's thoughts drifted to her children and the ranch. The looming question of what her life should look like moving forward pulled at her mind. The work in the garden usually brought her clarity, but today, it only seemed to underscore her confusion, even with Tally's advice. She just wanted to be sure that there would be stability for her and her children. Mike was a good person, and she had genuine feelings for him. But what she wanted and what was best for her children were at odds with one another.

Later, as dusk settled in and the air cooled, Leah joined Alice in the kitchen. The familiar routine of preparing dinner together offered a welcome distraction. The clattering of pots and pans, the sizzle of vegetables in the skillet, and the comforting scent of cooking filled the room, wrapping Leah in a cocoon of normalcy.

Alice, sensing Leah's quiet introspection, decided to break the silence.

"Leah, I'm sorry if I was too pushy earlier. I didn't mean to make things harder for you."

Leah looked up, her eyes softening. "It's okay, Alice. I know you mean well. It's just… everything's so complicated."

Alice nodded, her expression gentle and encouraging. "You can talk to me about it, you know. If you need to."

Leah took a deep breath, the words tumbling out before she could stop them.

"I do have feelings for Mike. I think about him a lot. But I'm scared, Alice. I'm scared of moving too fast, not being ready, of what my kids will think. And most of all, I'm scared of getting hurt again."

Alice placed a comforting hand on Leah's shoulder. "It's okay to be scared.

You've been through a lot. But don't let fear stop you from finding happiness. Mike seems like a good man, and he cares about you deeply. Maybe it's worth giving it a chance, even if it's just a small step at a time."

Leah nodded slowly, feeling a tiny spark of hope amidst the fear. "You're right. Maybe I do need to give it a chance. For now, I'll take it one day at a time and see where it leads."

Alice smiled, her eyes full of warmth. "That's all you can do. And remember, you're not alone in this. We're all here for you."

As they finished preparing dinner, Leah felt a sense of relief. Confiding in Alice had lightened her emotional burden, and she felt renewed resolve. Leah would take things one step at a time, allowing herself to think without being overwhelmed by fear. And she could find a way to open her heart again.

That night, as Leah sat on the edge of her bed, she said a little prayer for guidance. "Lord, if you are listening, please give me a sign. I don't want to be hurt again. I'm frightened, but I think I might like Mike. Please help me to know what's happening." She ended the prayer, and as she laid her head on her pillow, she thought about her late husband, Bobby, and how it was at the beginning of their relationship. There were a lot of the same emotions of excitement and the unknown. But she had fallen in love too quickly and later realized she regretted her mistake. As Leah closed her eyes and sleep took her, the visions of her and Bobby swirled through her dreams. She was woken up suddenly to the sound of her son Bobby Jr. Screaming, and as she shook the dream and the dread from her head, Leah made her way to the little room where Bobby and Sarah slept and gently reached for him. He was hot to the touch, and his body was sweaty. As Leah fumbled for the light switch, Alice walked in. "Alice, I think Bobby is sick. Can you call Susan and Doris, please?"

And then Leah began to look for the thermometer. Bobby's temperature was 104 degrees, and he was inconsolable. She began to strip him and put him in a tepid bath just as Susan and Doris arrived.

"I'm not sure what's wrong with him," Leah told them. "He seemed fine all day."

"Maybe he got too much sun." Susan offered.

"I don't know," Leah cried, "But he's burning up!"

"I can call the on-call pediatricians if you'd like," Alice offered. "That's who my parents always called in the middle of the night when I was sick."

"Yes, please," Leah answered desperately.

Alice quickly dialed the number for the on-call pediatrician while Leah held Bobby in the tepid bath, trying to soothe him. After a few rings, a calm and professional voice answered.

"Hello, Dr. Evans speaking; how can I help you?"

Alice explained the situation rapidly, detailing Bobby's high fever, inconsolable crying, and how he had been playing outside in the heat all day. Dr. Evans listened attentively before responding.

"First, let's try to bring his temperature down. It's good that you have him in a tepid bath. Continue with that for a few more minutes, then dry him off and dress him in light clothing. Avoid cold water or ice packs as they can cause shivering, which might raise his body temperature even more."

Leah could hear Alice repeating the instructions to the doctor, and she nodded to herself as she followed the advice. Bobby's cries were still heart-wrenching, but she could see some of the redness starting to leave his face.

Dr. Evans continued, "After the bath, give him an appropriate dose of acetaminophen or ibuprofen for his age and weight to help reduce the fever. Do you have either of those on hand?"

"Yes, we have both," Alice replied, looking to Leah, who nodded in confirmation.

"Good. Make sure to keep Bobby hydrated. Offer him small sips of water or an electrolyte solution frequently, but only force large amounts at once if he's up for it. Dehydration is common in these situations, especially with heat and physical activity."

Alice relayed this information, and Leah mentally noted to get Bobby to drink as soon as he was calm enough.

Dr. Evans then asked, "Does he have any other symptoms? Is he vomiting, having diarrhea, or showing any signs of severe lethargy or difficulty breathing?"

Alice looked at Leah, who shook her head. "No, just the high fever and crying," she answered for Leah.

"Alright," Dr. Evans said, "If his fever doesn't start to come down within an hour of giving him the medication, or if he starts showing other concerning symptoms, you should take him to the ER. It's important to monitor him closely tonight."

Feeling more in control, Leah thanked Alice for handling the call and took the phone. "Thank you, Dr. Evans. I really appreciate your help."

"Of course, Leah. Keep a close eye on him, and feel free to call back if things don't improve or if you're worried about anything. It's always better to be cautious."

Leah ended the call and looked at her son, whose cries had subsided to whimpers. She gently lifted him from the bath, dried him off, and dressed him in light pajamas. After giving him the recommended dose of acetaminophen, she held him close, whispering soothing words.

Susan and Doris stayed close by, offering moral support and watching Sarah, awakened by Bobby's screams and the frantic adult voices. Alice fetched a small cup of water and some electrolyte solution, and Leah got Bobby to take a few sips.

As the night wore on, Bobby's temperature gradually lowered, and he finally fell into an exhausted sleep in Leah's arms. She breathed a sigh of relief, grateful for her friends' support and Dr. Evans's guidance.

Leah's thoughts drifted back to her earlier prayer. Maybe this was the sign she needed—not a miraculous answer, but the strength and support to face whatever came her way. With her friends by her side and a cautious hope for the future, Leah felt a renewed determination to navigate her path, one step at a time.

The following day, the house was tranquil. Exhaustion had settled over everyone like a heavy blanket, and they all slept in, taking advantage of the calm after the chaotic night. Leah had fallen asleep in the rocking chair with Bobby still cradled in her arms, his little head resting on her shoulder. Susan and Doris had found places to sleep around the living room as they were too tired to return to their own house.

The loud ring of the phone abruptly shattered the tranquility, jolting everyone awake. Leah groggily rubbed her eyes, careful not to disturb Bobby, and reached for the phone.

"Hello?" she answered, her voice thick with sleep.

"Leah, it's Sheriff Morgan," came the familiar voice on the other end. "I'm sorry to call so early, but we have a situation. A woman and her child need a safe place to stay, and I was hoping we could bring them to your ranch."

Leah sat up straighter, fully awake now. "Of course, Sheriff. Bring them over. We'll get things ready."

As she hung up the phone, Leah looked around at her half-asleep friends. "That was Sheriff Morgan. He's bringing a woman and her child who need a safe place to stay. We need to get things in order."

The mention of someone in need was like an adrenaline shot to the group. Despite their exhaustion, they sprang into action, their tiredness replaced by a rush of energy and purpose.

Alice tidied up the living room, picking up blankets and pillows, while Susan headed to the kitchen to prepare breakfast and strong coffee. Doris grabbed clean linens and walked next door to the guest house, making sure it was welcoming and comfortable.

Leah gently placed Bobby in his crib. His fever was much lower, and his breathing was steady. She then joined the others, coordinating the efforts. "Let's ensure the child has toys and books at the guest house. Sarah, honey, can you help by picking out some of your things they might like?" she instructed. "And we should have some extra clothes ready, just in case." Sarah was eager to be included and began to search her room for some of her favorite toys.

The house buzzed with activity, the early morning light streaming through the windows. There was a sense of urgency but also a tangible excitement. Helping someone in need renewed the group's sense of purpose.

When the Sheriff's car pulled up the driveway, the ranch was ready to welcome its newest inhabitants. Leah and her friends stood on the porch, their hearts racing with anticipation and concern.

Sheriff Morgan exited the car and opened the door for the woman and her child. The woman looked tired and scared, clutching her child's hand tightly. Leah's heart went out to them immediately.

"Welcome," Leah said warmly, stepping forward. "I'm Leah, and this is Alice, Susan, and Doris. You're safe here. Come on inside."

The woman managed a weak smile, tears of relief in her eyes.

"Thank you so much. I'm Anna, and this is my daughter, Emily."

The group quickly felt at home as they entered the guest house. Susan offered Anna tea while Alice led Emily to meet Sarah, who was finishing the room Emily would stay in.

Sarah was so excited to show Emily the toys and books they had set out for her to play with. "This is my favorite dolly, but I'm letting her have a sleepover with you," Sarah offered. Emily was too shaken up and shy to speak, and tiny tears were seemingly about to escape her eyes.

In the living room, Leah sat down with Anna, her voice gentle and reassuring. "You're safe now, Anna. We're here to help however we can."

Anna nodded, her gratitude evident despite her exhaustion. "Thank you. I don't know what we would have done without you."

"We won't stay long, so you can settle in and get some rest," Doris offered. "We are just down the road there, and Leah and Alice live next door." She pointed out the window to the adjacent home.

The morning passed in a blur of activity as the ranch adapted to its new residents. Despite their tiredness, Leah and her friends found strength in their shared mission, their spirits lifted by the knowledge that they were making a difference.

The ranch settled into a new rhythm as the sun climbed higher in the sky. Tally cared for the animals as Sarah and Emily played near by. Sarah was thrilled to introduce her new friend to the chickens and the goats.

The sense of community and support was stronger than ever, and Leah felt deeply grateful for the people around her. Together, they faced the day's challenges, united by their compassion and determination to help those in need.

That night, a tired Leah crawled into bed. Her head barely hit the pillow before dreams took her to a familiar place. She was back with Bobby, and they had been fighting when he hit her. Then suddenly, Mike was in her dream, taking her hand and leading her to safety. Her heart was full of gratitude and love for rescuing her. She woke up when the sun began to peak through the bedroom window. It was time to let Mike know her feelings for him. She opened her phone and sent him a text message.

"Hi Mike, I hope this message finds you well. I've been thinking a lot lately and wanted to share some thoughts with you.

The other night had been incredibly tough, making me realize how precious and fragile life is. Your visit and conversation meant more to me than you could ever know. I've been so scared of moving forward, of letting someone into my heart again, but when I think of you, I feel something different. I feel hope, safety, and a gentle love I didn't know I could feel again.

You've been patient and understanding, giving me the space I needed but always being there when I needed you the most. Your kindness and support have been a beacon for me in these dark times, and I am deeply grateful.

I said I needed time, and I still do in some ways, but I also know I don't want to let fear dictate my life anymore. I want to explore this between us. I'm still scared, and there will be challenges, but we can face anything with you by my side.

Thank you for being the incredible person you are. I look forward to seeing where this journey takes us, step by step, together.

I'll see you this weekend, and we can talk more if you want. I'll talk to you soon! Leah"

A Lifeline

Mike was sitting in his squad car watching traffic when he got a text message from Leah. His heart was racing faster than the vehicles he was supposed to be watching. As he read each line repeatedly, his mind also began to run. He had been waiting for this moment, and he thought he would have to wait a long time. Just as he was about to reply, a Red pickup truck sped by him, clocking at 95 miles per hour. Mike immediately called it in as he began his pursuit. The occupant didn't seem to want to comply and sped up. Mike made another call to dispatch. "He's running! I need backup!"

As Mike began the chase, his Adrenaline kicked in. He knew this was dangerous, but the occupant slowed and pulled to the right.

"Occupant in the Red Truck, Put your hands on the steering wheel where I can see them, and do it right now!" Mike said with authority. But suddenly, the vehicle door opened as a 6-foot-5-inch man stepped out holding a shotgun. Mike didn't have time to respond and was shot. The shooter got back into his truck and sped off. Three passersby stopped to offer assistance, as his backup was also arriving on the scene. Mike was unconscious; the bullet had hit him in the neck.

Leah was making lunch and kept glancing at her phone, expecting to hear from Mike. She wasn't too worried yet, as she knew he was most likely busy with work. Alice could tell she seemed anxious and decided to ask her what was up.

"I see you glancing at your phone every five minutes. Is something wrong?"

"Hmmm…?" Leah asked, preoccupied with her thoughts.

"You have your head in the clouds now, and the soup is about to boil over!" Alice scolded.

"Ahhh!" "OH my gosh, you're right!" Leah jumped out of her daydream and began blowing on the pot to settle the liquid.

"So what gives girl? You have been floating through the day…" Alice asked, concerned.

Leah wasn't sure she wanted to tell anyone about her text message to Mike, but she looked at Alice and knew she needed to confide in her best friend.

"I sent a message to Mike this morning letting him know that I would be okay with starting a relationship."

Alice wasn't in the least surprised by Leah's admission. She tried to hide her glee and give Leah her support. "Hey, good for you! Is that why you keep looking at your phone?"

Leah blushed. "Yes, I thought I would have seen or heard anything by now, but he's probably busy at work."

Mike was Care-flighted to Parkland Hospital in Dallas, where the medical personnel swarmed around him, their movements precise and swift as they wheeled him through the corridors toward the operating room. Mike's condition was critical, and every second counted.

In the O.R., the trauma team sprang into action. Doctors and nurses collaborated seamlessly, each knowing their role in this life-saving effort. Mike was quickly assessed, and the extent of his injuries became apparent. The bullet penetrated his neck, causing severe damage to vital structures. Blood loss was significant, and immediate intervention was necessary to stabilize him.

The trauma surgeon took charge, barking out orders as the team mobilized. Instruments clattered, monitors beeped incessantly, and the room hummed with focused energy. Mike was swiftly intubated to secure his airway, ensuring he could breathe despite the trauma to his neck.

The surgical team faced the daunting task of repairing the damage caused by the gunshot wound. The bullet had torn through muscle, blood vessels, and possibly even nerves in Mike's neck. Delicate maneuvers were required to control bleeding and reconstruct the damaged tissues.

The team encountered challenges throughout the surgery that tested their skills and expertise. Complications arose, necessitating quick thinking and decisive action to keep Mike stable. Hours passed in tense silence as the surgery team worked fiercely to save Mike.

Finally, the surgeons emerged from the operating room after five hours of exhaustion etched on their faces. They approach Mike's Captain, John Henderson, their expression grave yet hopeful.

"The surgery was extensive," Doctor Foster, the lead, began, his voice tinged with weariness. "But we were able to repair the damage to Mike's neck. He's stable for now but not out of the woods yet. We'll need to monitor him closely in the ICU."

Captain Henderson felt relieved as he absorbed the news. "What is his prognosis going forward, Doc?" he asked.

The doctor took a moment to gather his thoughts before responding to Captain Henderson's inquiry. His expression shifted from weariness to professional focus as he addressed the Captain's question.

"Well, Mike's prognosis is guarded," the doctor began, his tone measured yet compassionate. "The surgery was successful in addressing the immediate threat to his life, but he's not out of danger yet. The bullet caused significant damage to his neck, and there may be lingering complications."

Captain Henderson nodded, absorbing the gravity of the situation. "What kind of complications are we looking at?" he asks, his voice tinged with concern.

The doctor adjusted his glasses, his gaze thoughtful as he considered his response. "Given the nature of the injury, there's a risk of complications such as infection, nerve damage, or even potential long-term impairment of his motor function or speech," he explained. "We'll need to closely monitor his condition in the ICU and conduct further tests to assess the extent of the damage."

John Henderson's jaw tightened at the mention of potential long-term consequences for Mike. He knew that the road to recovery would be arduous, but he remained determined to support his officer through every step of the journey.

"Thank you, Doctor," John said, his voice steady despite the underlying concern. "Please keep me updated on his condition. Mike is not just a member of my team; he's family and has no one else."

The doctor nodded reassuringly before excusing himself to attend to other patients. John watched the doctor go, his mind already turning to the challenges as he prepared to face the uncertain road ahead. John called dispatch to update them on Mike's condition. "Please let the rest of the team know, too. Mike is in capable hands, surrounded by a dedicated team of medical professionals committed to his recovery." The dispatcher, who had answered the Captain's call, was relieved.

As John walked out of the hospital, he was immediately surrounded by the press with cameras and lights in his face, with the media demanding answers for their six o'clock story.

It was dinner time, and Leah worried that Mike had changed his mind.

"Why hasn't he answered her," she thought to herself. She could hardly concentrate on the conversation that Sarah and Alice were having. "Mama! ARE YOU LISTENING TO ME!" Sarah demanded.

"I'm sorry, Honey," Leah startled out of her thoughts. "I am now. What are you asking me?"

"Alice wants to take me to town with her. She said there is a rodeo and that there will be some rides, too, and clowns! Can we go?" her daughter asked with anticipation.

"Oh, I guess so; I mean, if you are up to that, Alice?" Leah replied.

"Sure, I am. We will have so much fun, and it will give you a break for a few hours, too," Alice offered. Sarah danced up and down, chatting about how fun it would be.

There was a knock on the door; Susan and Doris walked in, their faces grave. As Susan and Doris entered the room, their somber expressions immediately caught Leah's attention. She felt a wave of unease wash over her as she watched them approach, her heart pounding. They had seen the six o'clock news and the information about Mike and the shooting. They didn't know that Leah had texted him earlier that morning. But they wanted the ladies to understand what had happened and that he wasn't coming to help with the fence after all.

Leah's stomach clenched with dread as she listened, her mind racing with a thousand terrible possibilities. She glanced at Alice, who offered her a reassuring hand squeeze before turning her attention back to Susan and Doris. Tears welled up in her eyes as she thought of Mike lying in a hospital bed, fighting for his life.

Alice moved closer, wrapping her arms around Leah in a comforting embrace. "We're here for you, Leah," she whispered, her voice filled with empathy. "Whatever you need, we're here to support you."

Leah clung to Alice, her heart aching with worry for Mike. "I need to see him," she said, her voice choked with emotion. I need to be there with him. Is he at Ennis?"

"No, Parkland in Dallas," Doris answered with concern. It will take you several hours to get there. Can you wait until tomorrow at least?"

Sarah looked up at her mother, her eyes wide with concern. "Can I come too, Mama?" she asked, her voice tinged with uncertainty.

"Not this time, baby. It is a long drive and will be way past your bedtime. Let Mama go this time, okay, honeybee?" Leah said, tears welling up.

Sarah nodded, her gaze lingering on her mother's face.

"You go ahead and go with Alice to the rodeo tomorrow just like we planned, Okay?" Leah said persuasively. And can you and Doris watch baby Bobby for me?" Leah asked, looking at Susan." I don't want to waste more time; I must see Mike tonight!"

"Sure, we will take care of him for you. Be careful, and please call us when you get there," Susan replied.

Leah nodded, her mind racing with thoughts of Mike as she gathered her belongings and prepared to journey to Dallas. With a heavy heart, she said her goodbyes to Sarah and Alice, promising to keep them updated on Mike's condition.

As Leah drove towards Parkland Hospital, her mind was filled with emotions. She couldn't shake the image of Mike lying unconscious in the ICU, fighting for his life. Tears streamed down her face as she grappled with the fear of what she might find when she arrived.

When Leah finally reached the hospital, she rushed through the corridors with a sense of urgency, her heart pounding. As she approached the ICU, she felt a knot form in her stomach, the gravity of the situation weighing heavily upon her.

Entering the ICU, Leah's eyes scanned the room until they landed on Mike's bed. Her breath caught in her throat as she saw him lying there, pale and motionless, surrounded by monitors and medical equipment. She felt a surge of anguish wash over her as she realized the extent of his injuries.

Moving closer to Mike's bedside, Leah reached out to gently take his hand, her fingers trembling with emotion. She whispered words of love and encouragement, hoping against hope that he could hear her and know she was there with him.

Suddenly, Leah felt a presence behind her and turned to see Captain Henderson standing in the doorway, his expression solemn as he watched her. Leah's heart skipped a beat as she recognized him, the memories of her past marriage to Bobby flooding back with painful clarity.

Captain Henderson approached her slowly, his gaze filled with empathy as he spoke. "Leah," he said softly, his voice filled with compassion. "I didn't realize you were still in touch with Mike."

Leah nodded, her eyes brimming with tears as she met his gaze. "He and I have started to care for one another, only just recently, as I was still mourning over my late husband's death," she admitted, her voice barely above a whisper. "And now, seeing him like this… it's breaking my heart; I think I waited too long, and now I am going to lose him too!" She sobbed.

Captain Henderson reached out to place a comforting hand on Leah's shoulder, his touch warm and reassuring. "I understand," he said gently. "And I'm here for you, whatever you need."

Leah felt a sense of gratitude wash over her as she looked into John Henderson's eyes, knowing she wasn't alone in her grief. Together, they stood by Mike's bedside, offering each other support and solace in the face of uncertainty.

Leah sat in the dimly lit hospital room, the only sound the steady beeping of the monitors connected to Mike. His face was ashen, a stark contrast to the vibrant man she had come to care for so deeply. Leah gently held his hand, her thumb brushing over his knuckles as if her touch could somehow transmit her strength to him. The weight of the past few days pressed heavily on her, a mix of fear that she had waited too long to tell Mike how she felt and an overwhelming sense of helplessness as she watched the machines keeping him alive with each mechanical breath.

Leah sighed as she looked at the clock on the wall. It read six o'clock in the morning. She reached for her phone and dialed home. She needed to hear her children's voices, to ground herself in the love and responsibility she felt for them. The phone rang twice before Doris answered.

"Leah, how are you?" Doris's voice was filled with concern.

"I'm… managing," Leah replied, her voice trembling slightly. "How are the kids?"

"They're okay. They miss you, but we are taking good care of them, And Alice will be taking Sarah to the rodeo in a few hours."

Leah's heart ached. "I miss them too. But I need to stay with Mike for a few more days if you all can manage? It's a long drive back to Hamilton, and I can't leave him like this."

There was a pause. "Leah, you need to think about the kids. They need their mom."

"I know, Doris. I know. But Mike needs me too. He's in a coma. What if he wakes up and I'm not here?"

Susan's voice came on the line, filled with gentle urgency. "Leah, we understand how much Mike means to you. But your children need their mother. We're just worried about how long you'll be away."

Leah felt a pang of hurt. "Do you think I'm not considering them? Of course I am. But Mike… I have to tell him…"

"We're not saying you don't care about your kids, Leah," Susan said softly. "We just want you to find a balance. Maybe it's time to come home, even if it's just for a little while."

Leah's resolve wavered. "I don't know if I can do that. I need to be here for Mike."

John Henderson, sitting quietly in the other chair, cleared his throat. "Leah, I need to get back to Ennis, but I promise I'll check on Mike for you. I'll make sure he's taken care of."

Leah looked at him, her eyes brimming with gratitude and despair. "Thank you, Captain Henderson. That means a lot."

John nodded and said, "Please call me John. It seems we are family now." Leah smiled back at him and told Doris and Susan she wasn't leaving Mike yet, and her mind was made up. She hung up her phone with a slight feeling of guilt and anger rising within. Her thoughts were jumbled, and she found it hard to concentrate. She looked at Mike, her heart breaking. She knew Doris and Susan were right, but the idea of leaving Mike tore at her.

Three days passed in a blur of worry and exhaustion. Leah barely left Mike's side, talking to him, hoping he could hear her. As she rested her head on the edge of Mike's bed, Susan and Doris arrived unannounced. Leah was surprised but relieved to see them.

"We couldn't let you stay here alone any longer," Susan said, wrapping Leah tightly in a hug. "You need to come home, even if it's just for a little while."

Leah hesitated, glancing back at Mike. "I don't want to leave him."

Doris took her hand. "We know. But you need to take care of yourself too. The kids need their mom."

Leah nodded, tears streaming down her face. "Okay. I'll come home. But I want to come back as soon as I can. I need to be here when he wakes up."

Susan and Doris exchanged relieved glances. "Of course, Leah. We'll make sure you get back here."

They all spent a few more hours with Mike, Leah holding his hand, talking to him, and promising she would be back. She hoped he could hear her, that her words were reaching him somehow.

As she prepared to leave, she kissed his forehead gently. "I'll be back, Mike. I promise."

In his coma, Mike heard her. Her words were like a lifeline, pulling him through the darkness. He tried to move, to let her know he understood, but his body wouldn't cooperate. He was trapped in the dream, aware but unable to act.

Leah walked out of the hospital with Susan and Doris, her heart heavy but determined. She would return to her children, but she would also return to Mike. Leah had to be there when he woke, telling him how much he meant to her.

As they drove away, Leah looked back at the hospital in her rear-view mirror, a silent promise in her heart. She would be back—for Mike, her children, and herself.

Love In Bloom

Mike woke up from his coma after several intense weeks of constant vigil by Leah, John, and other members of the Ennis Police Force.

Once Mike was stable enough, he was moved to a rehab center in Ennis under the watchful eye of John Henderson. John rarely left his side except when duty called, and Mike's coworkers visited often to cheer him up.

But his favorite visits were from Leah and her children. Leah made it a point to visit him three times a week, bringing different snacks or meals to break up the monotony of the rehab center's bland food. The children would play quietly, sometimes finding amusement in pressing the controls on the bed, causing it to move up and down. Leah would scold them for playing too much, but Mike always encouraged them, finding joy in their laughter. Watching the children playing with so much joy and zest for life seemed healing. He welcomed the distraction and found new meaning since the shooting.

One day, Mike confided in John about that dark and terrifying moment that forever changed him. "John, you know that day?" Mike began, his voice trembling, "When I was shot, I saw my own body slumped over in my car. The paramedics were working frantically to bring me back. It was surreal and terrifying, like watching a movie where you're the main character but utterly powerless." He paused, Mike's eyes glistening with un-shed tears. "But what really shook me to my core was what happened afterward. While I was in the coma, I could hear everyone's voices— you and Leah, the doctors and nurses. I could hear your prayers, and fears, and your hopes. I wanted so desperately to reach out, to tell everyone I was there, that I could hear you, but I couldn't move or speak. I felt trapped in a void between life and death, and it still haunts me!"

John listened intently, his heart aching for his friend. "That must have been incredibly isolating," he said thoughtfully. John was a Christian but had wandered away from his faith because of all the long hours of working and the hard things he saw. But he had begun to pray again while Mike was in the coma. He didn't realize that Mike could hear him.

"It was," Mike replied, "but it was also… enlightening in a way. In that silent darkness, I felt a presence, something beyond this world. It was as if God was there with me, holding me in His hands. I realized how fragile life is and how every moment is a gift. It made me see things differently. I don't take anything for granted anymore. Every breath, every heartbeat, it's all a blessing."

John nodded, his own eyes moist. "I believe you. Sometimes, it takes a brush with death to truly appreciate the miracle of life. What you went through sounds like you were given a second chance, a new perspective."

"Exactly," Mike said, his voice gaining strength. "And I don't want to waste it. I've started praying more, connecting with my faith. It's become a cornerstone of my life now. I feel like I was given a glimpse into something beyond our understanding, a reminder that there's more to our existence than just the physical world. It's given me a sense of peace and purpose."

John reached out and placed a comforting hand on Mike's shoulder. "I'm glad you shared that with me. Your experience is a powerful reminder for us all to cherish our lives and our connections."

Mike smiled, a mixture of relief and gratitude washing over him. "Thank you for listening. It means more than you know. You have been like a brother to me." John returned the sentimental gesture. He told Mike that they were family. And that he wouldn't abandon him.

Leah's devotion to Mike was unwavering. It had been hard for her children, as she had split her time between them and Mike while he remained at Parkland Hospital. When he was brought out of his coma five weeks after the shooting,

Leah was there, holding his hand, grateful she could finally tell him how she felt. Her love for him had grown into full bloom during those vigil days. Even in his comatose state, Mike, aware of her diligence and devotion, felt his feelings for her deepen. Leah's selflessness in caring for Mike, despite the challenges, was a testament to her compassion and dedication.

The morning he was removed from the medical coma, Mike saw Leah as beautiful as the first day he had met her. He knew he wanted to marry her but focused on his recovery first. He didn't want to be a burden; he wanted to care for her and her children.

The doctors were hopeful he would return to light duty. Though he might never patrol again, he could help with lighter tasks at the department. John Henderson arranged for Mike to transfer to the Detectives unit. Although initially disappointed, Leah helped Mike see the value in this new arrangement. This new role would give him more time to spend with her, catching up on the time lost during his recovery.

Mike worked hard to regain his strength, pushing himself to be released from rehab sooner than expected. Six months later, Mike was feeling optimistic. He was ready to go home thanks to his colleagues and Leah's love and support. Mike's determination and resilience were evident in his relentless efforts to recover and return home.

Leah sat on the porch of her ranch house, looking out at the guest homes scattered across the property. The sun was setting, casting a warm glow over the fields. She took a deep breath, knowing the conversation she was about to have would be difficult but necessary. She heard footsteps behind her and turned to see Doris and Susan approaching.

"Leah, what's on your mind?" Doris asked, sensing her friend's unease.

Leah gestured for them to sit. "I've been thinking a lot about Mike and his recovery," she began, her voice heavy with emotion. "He's being released soon, and I want to suggest that he stays in one of the guest homes here on the ranch."

Susan glanced at Doris before speaking. "Leah, we support you, but those guest homes are for women in need. We've had a steady flow of guests over the past few months. How would this work?"

Leah nodded, understanding their concerns. "I know it's unconventional, but Mike still needs care, and I can provide that for him here. It would only be temporary until he's fully recovered and can return to light duty with his department."

Doris leaned forward, her brow furrowed. "What about the women who need those homes? We can't just turn them away."

"I've thought about that," Leah said earnestly. "We can make arrangements to accommodate them elsewhere on the property. Maybe in the main house, or even set up temporary housing if needed. This is important to me. Mike risked his life in the line of duty, and he saved mine. I owe it to him to help now."

Susan sighed, her expression softening. "Leah, we know how much you care about Mike. But are you sure you're not letting your feelings cloud your judgment? This is a big responsibility."

Leah's eyes filled with tears. "I love him, Susan. And yes, my feelings are involved, but that doesn't change the fact that he needs care. He's done so much for me, for all of us. I can't bear the thought of him struggling on his own."

Doris reached out and took Leah's hand. "We understand that, Leah. We do. But we must ensure this is the best decision for everyone involved. What if things don't go as planned?"

Leah squeezed Doris's hand, her voice trembling. "I'm willing to take that risk. I've seen how far he's come, and I know he can fully recover with the right support. Please, just give him a chance. Give us a chance."

Susan looked at Doris, then back at Leah. "Alright, Leah. If you believe this is best for Mike, we'll support you. We'll make it work somehow. But we must stay flexible and ensure the women we help aren't neglected."

Leah's face lit up with relief and gratitude. "Thank you, both of you! I promise I'll make sure everything runs smoothly. Mike needs this, and so do I."

Doris smiled gently. "We trust you, Leah. Let's figure out the logistics and ensure everyone is cared for."

Susan nodded in agreement. "We'll help you every step of the way. Let's do this together."

Leah felt a weight lift off her shoulders as she hugged her two friends.

The week that Mike moved in was a blur of excitement and frenzy. Leah wanted to make Mike feel at home, but she couldn't decide how to arrange the furniture to best accommodate him as he was still using a wheelchair temporarily. She had also added tiny feminine touches like drapery and comfortable pillows bedecked with floral print and warm throws for cooler evenings, should he want to cover up. Tally was also enjoying the camaraderie. She and Leah also formed a sweet bond while Mike fought for his life. She had taken to the children, helping to watch them when Leah was away, often while caring for Mike in the hospital, going so far as to adopt them as her grandchildren. They also adored her.

Tally busied herself in the kitchen, organizing the fridge with ready-to-eat meals that she and Susan had prepared so that Mike would not need to cook for himself while recuperating. "I think he will enjoy my enchiladas. My Fred loved these," She went on, a nostalgic look in her eyes. "And he loved my buttercream cake too, I baked several for Mike, and they freeze well, so he will never want, Oh, I miss my Fred!" Suddenly, Tally was crying as she often did; her dementia was progressing quickly, and no one knew when Tally would burst into tears.

But Leah had a way to redirect her with gentle respect and tact. "Tally, you know I just remembered I left the tablecloth in a box in the bedroom. Would you be a dear and fetch it for me?" Leah chirped as she squeezed Tally's hand to reassure her. And just like that, Tally rallied like a small child might and happily left her task in the kitchen to look for the tablecloth. She came back shortly, and she and Leah laid it on the small dining room table. The tiny home was now ready to receive its inhabitant.

Mike was very humbled when Doris and Susan asked him to move onto the property. They decided to ask him to come on as a foreman and protector so as not to diminish his ego and make him feel like a burden. Mike was grateful for their thoughtfulness. And since it meant being closer to Leah, he wasn't about to decline.

The small home was comfortable, and soon, Mike found a new rhythm. He was still limited in what he could do to help around the ranch, but he did make himself useful. All of the women soon began to respect him and rely on his judgment when it came to things like building a fence or a goat shed. As he gained more strength He was able to add his weight to the heavy lifting. The work helped in his recuperating faster.

The weeks passed quickly, and Mike's bond with Leah deepened. He felt a sense of belonging he hadn't felt before. They spent more time together, and his feelings for her grew more assertive.

But when Mike returned to work, he didn't want to leave the ranch or Leah. Their bond had become unbreakable. With the help of Susan, Alice, Doris, John, and Leah's kids, Mike planned a heartfelt marriage proposal.

One sunny afternoon, Mike gathered everyone from the ranch to join him at Ruston Cattle Company, where his old coworkers also gathered. Leah was surprised to see their friends there, but Mike dropped to one knee before she could ask.

"Leah, these past few months have shown me what's truly important. Your love and support have been my strength. I can't imagine my life without you. Will you marry me?"

Leah's eyes filled with tears. "Yes, Mike. A thousand times, yes!"

Cheers erupted as Mike slipped a ring onto her finger. They embraced, surrounded by their loved ones, feeling complete.

Mike requested reassignment to the Hamilton Police Department as a dispatcher until he could return as an officer. The department approved it under the special circumstances.

A quick justice-of-the-peace wedding was arranged, and Leah and Mike were married, surrounded by their close friends and family.

Alice was sad to lose her roommate but so excited for Leah's new happiness as she stood at the window of the tiny house she once shared with Leah, watching as the last rays of the sun cast a golden glow over the fields; she felt a bittersweet mix of emotions, knowing that her dear friend Leah was embarking on a new chapter of her life. She sighed softly, remembering all the moments they had shared as roommates. It was hard to say goodbye to that chapter, but she couldn't help but feel excited for Leah's happiness with Mike.

Leah came up behind Alice and wrapped her arms around her warmly. "Thank you for everything, Alice. You've been my rock through all of this."

Alice smiled, a tear slipping down her cheek. "I'm so happy for you, Leah. Mike is a good man, and you two deserve all the happiness in the world."

They stood silently for a moment, the weight of the past and the promise of the future hanging between them. Then, Leah pulled back, her eyes sparkling with excitement.

"Mike and I are moving into the tiny home right next to you, so you can't get too far away from me! Leah said, a mischievous glint in her eye. We do plan to build another home nearby once he's fully recovered. But for now, it means we are neighbors, even if we can't be roommates!"

Alice laughed. "I'll miss having you as my roommate, but I'm excited to have you as a neighbor. And who knows, maybe I'll get a new roommate, and we will all become great friends."

Sanctuary

In the following weeks, the ranch's guest homes filled up, and the need for support and donations was greater than ever. One evening, a new guest arrived—a young woman named Maria who had fled an abusive relationship. She was quiet and reserved, but Alice could see the determination in her eyes. With its warm and welcoming atmosphere, the ranch was a beacon of hope for Maria, providing a safe space for her to heal and grow.

As Alice showed Maria to the room where she would be staying, Alice felt a sense of purpose. "This is your new home," Alice said warmly. We're all here to support each other."

Maria smiled tentatively. "Thank you. It means a lot to have a safe place to stay."

Alice nodded, knowing that this was just the beginning.

The ranch was becoming more than just a stopover for her; it was a diverse Community where people from all walks of life found strength, friendship, and a chance to start anew.

Leah and Mike's love story had brought them all together, but now it was time for everyone to write their own stories. As Alice closed the door to her room that night, she felt a renewed sense of hope. The future was bright, and the possibilities were endless.

Maria needed to figure out her living arrangement. Every day was a new lesson in how to trust. Her life had been one of turmoil and fear. So, she was still not sure how to relate to others in a meaningful way. She spent the first few days either in her room with her door locked or alone around the ranch. Leah's children, however, who were not shy, managed to warm their way into her heart and chip away at some of the ice still left from her harrowing experiences. Children often saw her as a beacon of light and were drawn to her like a moth to a flame. And she welcomed their company when they would find her hiding from the others.

One sunny afternoon, Maria sat on the porch, an unopened book in her lap. The gentle sounds of laughter floated through the air as Leah's children played in the yard. Their carefree energy was infectious, and for the first time, Maria felt a flicker of something she hadn't experienced in a long while: curiosity. It was a small but significant turning point in her healing journey, a testament to the impact of the supportive community around her.

Just then, Sarah bounded over, her cheeks flushed with excitement. "Hi! Wanna play?"

Maria hesitated, the walls she had built around herself feeling heavy. "Um, I don't think I can right now," she replied softly, her voice barely above a whisper.

Sarah's smile faltered momentarily, but then she plopped beside Maria. "You can just watch! It's super fun!"

As the girl chattered on, Maria felt warmth in her chest. She watched some other children at the ranch run and tumble, their laughter ringing like music. Each giggle seemed to draw her out of her reclusiveness and wear down her reluctance, reminding her of the innocence she had longed to protect in her life.

The next day, Maria found herself joining them in the yard. It started with just sitting on the sidelines, but Sarah had dragged her into a game of tag with the other children before she knew it. With each laugh and playful chase, Maria felt a part of herself awaken. The joy was foreign yet exhilarating, and she realized that perhaps there was room for healing amid the chaos. With their innocent laughter and carefree energy, the children played a significant role in Maria's healing journey, helping her rediscover the joy of life.

In the evenings, as the sun dipped below the horizon, casting a warm glow over the ranch, Alice would often find Maria on the porch, reflecting on her day. "You look happier," Alice noted one evening, leaning against the railing.

Maria nodded, her heart swelling with a mix of hope and uncertainty. "The kids… they make it easier," she admitted. "I forgot what it felt like to be… free."

Alice smiled, her eyes sparkling with understanding. "It's okay to let yourself feel joy again. You're not alone here."

With each passing day, Maria began to venture out more, sharing small bits of her past with Alice and gradually opening up to the other guests. Each story she shared was a step toward reclaiming her life, and with every shared laughter and tear, she discovered that vulnerability could lead to connection.

One evening, as a group of women sat around a fire pit, roasting marshmallows, Maria listened to others recount their struggles and victories. Their stories resonated with her, and she felt a powerful sense of belonging she hadn't thought possible. It was as if she had found a missing piece of herself in this circle of shared experiences.

"Maybe I can tell my story too," she whispered to Alice, who sat beside her.

"Absolutely. When you're ready," Alice replied, gently encouraging squeezing her hand.

As the flames danced in the darkness, Maria looked around at the faces lit by the firelight—hopeful, determined, and united in their journey. The ranch was no longer just a refuge; it was a sanctuary of healing, a safe haven from the storms of life, a canvas for new beginnings, and she was ready to paint her own story, stroke by stroke.

One evening, Alice and Maria stood side by side in their tiny kitchen, the comforting aroma of dinner filling the air. Maria sliced vegetables, her movements careful and precise, while Alice stirred a pot on the stove. They chatted softly, the conversation a soothing backdrop to their tasks. For Maria, these simple, everyday activities were a welcome relief from the chaos of her past life.

Maria looked up, her eyes filled with gratitude. "Alice, I can't thank you enough for everything. This place has given me a chance to breathe again."

Alice smiled warmly. "You're part of our family now, Maria. We're all here for each other."

Suddenly, the tranquility of the evening was shattered by the sound of a car engine revving loudly outside, breaking into the peace that was normal in their rural setting. Alice and Maria exchanged a worried glance, their hearts beginning to race. They both knew by a shared intuition the potential dangers that lurked outside their walls.

As the engine cut off, heavy footsteps echoed across the porch. The front door burst open, and there stood Jose, Maria's abusive husband. His face was twisted with anger, his eyes wild as he scanned the room.

"Maria!" he bellowed. "You think you can hide from me?"

Maria's face went pale, and she stepped back, her hands trembling. "Jose, please, just leave!" She cried.

Alice quickly stepped between Maria and Jose, with her arms stretched out as if to block Jose and protect Maria. Her voice was steady despite the fear coursing through her. "You need to leave now. This is private property!"

Jose sneered, taking a menacing step forward. "Stay out of this. She's my wife. She comes with me!" He spat.

But Alice was determined to protect her new friend. She raised her chest higher and jutted her chin forward. "I said leave...NOW!" She said with a firm, deep voice of authority as she pointed to their front door, her eyes blazing with resolve and bravado.

Before Jose could lift his fist to Alice, Mike appeared in the doorway, his presence commanding and calm, his sidearm in one hand. Though he was still recovering, his instincts as a police officer were as sharp as ever. He was leaning on his cane with his other hand but also calculating his next step as he planned to deter Jose from harming the two women.

"That's enough!" Mike said firmly, stepping into the kitchen. "You're trespassing. Leave now, or I'll call the police."

Jose's eyes flicked to Mike, sizing him up. "And who the hell are you?" he mocked, as he could see that Mike was leaning heavily on his cane. Despite the pistol in his other hand, Jose didn't feel the need to comply.

"I'm Mike from next door," he said, his voice unwavering, his eyes locked tight onto Jose's

There was a flicker of hesitation in Jose's eyes, but his anger flared, "You have no right to interfere here asshole! Maria is my wife, and I am taking her back with me now!" He threatened as he advanced towards Mike. But when Mike dropped his cane and raised his gun towards Jose, he knew he was outmatched. "You think you can stop me?" he spat, with one last attempt to manipulate the situation, though he knew he was out matched.

Mike took a step closer, his posture strong and authoritative. "Yes, I do. Leave now or face the consequences!"

The tension in the room was obvious, the air thick with fear and determination. Maria clutched Alice's arm, her heart pounding in her chest. She had never felt so scared yet so protected.

Finally, Jose seemed to realize he was beaten. He snarled one last threat, "This isn't over," He pointed at Maria before turning and storming past Mike out of the house.

The sound of his car peeling away faded into the distance, leaving a heavy silence behind.

Mike turned to Maria and Alice, his expression softening. "Are you both okay?"

Maria nodded, sobbing now, with tears streaming down her face. "Thank you, Mike. I was so scared. I didn't know what to do."

Alice hugged Maria tightly. "You're safe now, Maria. He won't come back."

Later that evening, Doris and Susan arrived after hearing about the incident. They found Mike on the porch, still on high alert but with a sense of relief washing over him.

"Mike," Doris began, her voice thick with emotion. "We can't thank you enough. You handled that situation perfectly."

Susan nodded, tears in her eyes. "We always worry about something like this happening. Knowing you're here makes all the difference."

Mike shook his head, his humility shining through. "I just did what needed to be done. We're all in this together, and I'm glad I could help."

Doris placed a hand on Mike's arm, her gratitude evident. "You did more than help, Mike. You protected us. That means everything."

Mike's bravery made the ranch feel safer and more secure as the night settled in. The women knew they needed to be more prepared, and Mike suggested they have a safety meeting the following morning.

After breakfast, they gathered at Mike and Leah's home to discuss the previous night's ordeal and determine how to prevent it from happening again.

"I think we need to start with tighter security at the road with a gate at the beginning of the driveway and a second checkpoint closer to the houses. And we need to invest in cameras too. A few down at the first gate and then some at the second one. We can also add additional ones on each of the outsides of the homes on the property. Either the doorbell kind or motion-activated ones on the corners of the houses just so we see who is coming around." Mike suggested that Doris and Susan have their team members invest in the cameras, and he would talk to his friend John about other security measures.

"I agree with Mike," Susan offered. We got too complacent and let our guard down too soon. We need to step up our game. Last night rattled me to the core!"

"I had a hard time sleeping too," Doris admitted, "Mike, if you hadn't been here, I do not know what we would have done!"

"Well, Ladies, that is my next discussion. I will be able to return to patrol in a few weeks. And my schedule will be a lot more restrictive. I won't be around as much and won't be home later in the evenings when most of these crimes might occur. Now, I have already spoken to Leah, and she is in agreement at least here in our home, we will be putting in a gun safe, and I will be teaching Leah how to use a gun properly. It will be secured away from the children. As a police officer, I have to have one on my person anyway, so we will already have one in this home. I am getting Leah her own. If you want to learn how to defend yourself and are comfortable, I would like to be the one to teach you how to defend yourself and your own property."

"Mike, I am very unsure," Doris began, "I just don't know how I feel about guns on the property; while I know you have to have your assigned sidearm, and this is your home, I can't say that I agree that Leah should have one too, I know this is your home, but you rent from us. This is our property, and I have always felt guns weren't the answer to anything."

"I understand your concern, Doris," Mike agreed with her, "But this is my home, as a tenet yes, we are under your authority, I get it, But I will not let what happened last night come to my wife or children. We cannot let our feelings get in the way of the facts. Of course, I can see your point. But bad guys won't! They aren't going to care that you have a disdain for guns or are against them. They will be all the more happy to use one against you. I won't allow that to happen to my family, period!" Mike ended his speech.

"Okay, I have to agree with Mike, Doris," Susan butted in, "I am with you that I am extremely and I mean extremely against guns. I fear them!" She confessed, "But last night shows us we are unprepared for what could happen. Jose could have shot Maria, Alice, or even Mike. He could have come after all of us! And so I want to know that I am prepared; Mike, will you help me pick out a suitable piece for my personal protection and teach me to use it, please?"

Mike was too happy to oblige and told the ladies he would gladly offer any assistance. Ultimately, all but Doris agreed to learn to protect themselves and their Community on the ranch. Doris needed more time to think this wild new concept over. In the meantime, she contacted her Ennis team to get ready to hold another gala so that they could raise funds for the cameras and gates they would need to secure the perimeter.

While at work later in the week, Mike called on his friend John to meet with him to discuss more security measures and have him start an investigation into how Jose found Maria at the ranch. Her whereabouts were supposed to have been sealed.

Mike met John at a local diner. They sat in a corner booth, away from prying ears. John had a reputation for being meticulous and thorough, qualities Mike admired and trusted.

"John, I need your help," Mike began, leaning in closer. "We had a serious security breach at the ranch. Jose Hernandez, Maria's abusive husband, found her. It's a miracle no one got hurt. We need to figure out how he knew her whereabouts."

John frowned, his mind already working through the possibilities. "That information should have been sealed. Are you thinking there's a leak?"

"Has to be," Mike nodded. "We need to trace it back to its source. This isn't just about Maria. The ranch offers sanctuary to women in danger. If one person's information got out, others might be at risk too."

John tapped his fingers on the table thoughtfully. "I'll start digging. We'll check the usual channels first – courthouse, police records, and any place her info might have been stored. It could be something as simple as a clerical error or something more sinister."

As John began his investigation, Mike focused on implementing the new security measures at the ranch. The first gate went up at the driveway entrance, with cameras monitoring every vehicle approaching. The second checkpoint was installed closer to the houses, ensuring another layer of protection.

In addition to the gates and cameras, Mike and John designed a security protocol for the ranch Community. They also held training sessions on situational awareness, self-defense, and emergency response plans. Though initially hesitant, the women at the ranch began to feel empowered and more in control of their safety.

Days turned into weeks, and the ranch became a fortress of safety and solidarity. John's investigation uncovered a disturbing truth: there was indeed a leak within a government department that had handled Maria's case. A disgruntled employee, angry over a demotion, had sold confidential information to make a quick profit. The leak was not limited to Maria's case; it could potentially expose countless others who sought protection.

Armed with this information, Mike and John coordinated with the authorities to ensure the leak was sealed and the responsible party was brought to justice. Maria's case was prioritized, and additional measures were taken to protect her identity and location. Jose was picked up on charges of breaking his parole and also not following the restraining order. He wouldn't be a threat to their Community any longer.

One evening, as the sun set over the ranch, casting a golden glow on the landscape, all the residents gathered for a meeting. Mike stood before them, a sense of pride and gratitude filling his heart.

"We've come a long way," he began, his voice steady. "What happened was a wake-up call. But we've faced it head-on, and we're stronger for it. We've built something here, something that can't easily be torn down."

Alice, standing beside Maria, nodded in agreement. "We've learned to protect ourselves and each other. This ranch isn't just a place to hide but to heal and grow stronger."

Maria, her eyes filled with tears of gratitude, stepped forward. "I owe my life to all of you. You've given me more than just a safe place; you've given me a family. I'll never be able to thank you enough."

As the meeting concluded, the women of the ranch felt a renewed sense of hope and determination.

Ultimately, the ranch became a sanctuary and a symbol of resilience and empowerment. While the threats they faced were relevant, so was their unwavering commitment to protecting and supporting one another.

Buckles and Bows

Doris and Susan were going over their monthly budgets for the ranch operation. They had been running steadily for over two years, with many women entering the program, some staying on long-term, and many rotating out. There were a few who came and had to come back a few more times because they found it hard to leave their abusive situations at first. Doris suggested that everyone who entered the program register for free counseling sessions to mitigate repeat stays. The ranch aimed to empower women to make tough choices and stand on their own two feet. Alice and Leah had returned to school to become licensed councilors, and the nonprofit set up through the ranch paid their wages to support the women who cycled through. They could now contribute to their daily expenses and not depend on the ranch's generosity.

As Doris and Susan were balancing the books, an unexpected knock on their door came. To their surprise, it was Alphonse, Alice's father. He had visited his daughter and stopped to see how everyone was doing.

"I hope y'all aren't too busy; I was in the neighborhood," He chuckled

"Absolutely not; now you hug my neck, Alphonse," Doris said as she let him in. "Susan and I are just looking over our books and about to take a break."

"How are you two getting on these days?" Alphonse asked genuinely

"Well, we have seen better numbers than this, I will admit," Susan said, blowing some air out of her mouth. "We haven't quite figured out how to profit with the ranch.

So far, we are in the red and only stay afloat with the donations. But we can't always count on them to be consistent."

Alphonse listened intently and told the ladies Alice had filled him in on the dilemma. He wanted to offer his expert advice if they wanted it.

"So I see you are taking on cattle now," He observed, "And how many have you sold?"

"None yet," Doris said. But we are trying to. I mean, we think we understand the how of it." She went on, "We have hired a few ranch hands who assured us that they know the cattle business. But they haven't told us when we need to sell or where. I know we have a good stock out there." She said, gazing out the window toward the pasture.

Alphonse nodded thoughtfully, his weathered face betraying years of experience in the cattle business. "Well, ladies, let me tell you a few things that might help," he began. "Timing is everything in this business; it's a cutthroat industry! You need to know the market cycles. Prices for cattle can fluctuate quite a bit depending on the season, the feed prices, and the general market demand. Generally speaking, the best time to sell cattle is in the spring or early summer when the demand for beef is high. But you should always monitor the market trends and adjust your selling times accordingly."

Susan and Doris listened attentively, nodding as they absorbed the information.

"Another thing," Alphonse continued, "is to ensure your cattle are in top condition before selling them. Buyers are always willing to pay more for healthy, well-fed cattle. Make sure they have a good diet and are stress-free. This will improve their weight and overall quality, which fetches a higher price."

Doris jotted down notes, glancing at Susan, who looked equally impressed by Alphonse's knowledge.

"And don't forget about diversification," Alphonse added. "Don't put all your eggs in one basket. Alongside cattle, you might want to consider other streams of income. Maybe some sheep or more goats will be needed. You might even consider a small dairy operation. Diversifying can help cushion against market fluctuations in the beef industry."

"That's great advice, Alphonse," Susan said. "We hadn't really considered diversification."

Alphonse smiled warmly. "I'm glad to be of help. Now, about your financial situation, I have an idea. I've been thinking about ways to support your incredible work here. How about we set up a matching donation program? For every dollar the Community donates, I'll match it. Let it run for a year and see how much better you are doing. This way, we can double the impact of each donation." He paused to let his suggestion sink in. The women were astonished by Alphonse's generosity.

"Additionally, I'd like to propose a fundraiser event – a ranch fair. We can invite the town, have games, sell homemade goods, and showcase the ranch. This could not only raise funds but also raise awareness about what you're doing here."

Doris and Susan exchanged excited looks. "That sounds amazing, Alphonse," Doris said, her eyes sparkling with hope. "It would really give us a boost."

"Absolutely," Susan agreed. "And a ranch fair could bring the community together and show them firsthand the positive impact we're making."

"Exactly," Alphonse said, smiling. "I'll help you plan it, and we can get the ball rolling immediately. Let's ensure this ranch survives and thrives, giving every woman here the best chance at a new beginning."

As the three of them continued to discuss the details, the room buzzed with renewed energy and optimism. Alphonse's visit, filled with practical advice and a generous offer, injected a much-needed hope and excitement into the ranch's future. His support was a clear demonstration of the power of community in empowering these women to create a new beginning for themselves.

One afternoon, a few days later, while Doris and Susan were excitedly planning the "Ranch A-fair," Leah stopped over to let them in on her news.

She was expecting a baby! The two older women were ecstatic and beside themselves with joy. So much had changed for all three of them since they had moved onto the ranch. And now, more fantastic news, with new life on the way, everything was falling into place just as Doris had dreamed it all would. The shared joy of this new life, a testament to the strength and resilience of the community, filled the room with warmth and camaraderie.

"Well, on top of a ranch fair, we need to start planning a baby shower too!" Susan exclaimed. "Do you have a due date yet?" She asked.

"My doctor thinks around Thanksgiving," Leah said, glowing

"Well, that's the perfect time to be born, and we sure will be giving tons of thanks to God for this new little life," Doris added with pride.

"I wanted to see if we could include a gender reveal at the ranch fair," Leah asked hopefully.

"I don't see why not," Susan said, looking at Doris thoughtfully. "All our friends will already be here, which makes perfect sense. What do you think, Doris?" She asked, still looking at her long-time friend.

Doris had a light bulb moment and a huge smile on her face. "I know just the kind of gender reveal surprise, too! " she exclaimed. Doris's eyes twinkled with excitement as she explained her idea. "How about a cowboy or cowgirl-themed gender reveal?" she said, her smile widening. We can incorporate it into the ranch fair seamlessly," Doris paused to gather her thoughts, while Leah and Susan waited expectantly.

"Picture this: we have a big hay bale setup in the fairground, decorated with cowboy boots, hats, and lassos. We'll set up two big barrels – one labeled 'cowboys' and the other 'cowgirls' – and let the guests vote on what they think the baby will be."

Leah and Susan looked intrigued, leaning in as Doris continued. "Now, for the big reveal, we can have a large, decorated box filled with either blue or pink balloons. We'll place the box on a hay wagon and hitch it to a horse-drawn cart. At the right moment, Leah and Mike can climb up on the wagon and pull the string together to release the balloons. It'll be a beautiful and exciting way to reveal the baby's gender, with everyone gathered around, cheering and celebrating."

"That's brilliant, Doris!" Leah exclaimed, clapping her hands. "I love the idea of including everyone in the reveal, and the horse-drawn cart is such a perfect touch."

"And we can have fun activities leading up to the reveal," Susan added.

"Maybe a sack race, a lasso contest, and even a petting zoo for the kids. It'll be a wonderful day for the whole community."

Doris nodded enthusiastically. "Yes, and we can have a country band playing music, line dancing, and lots of good food. We'll make it a day to remember, not just for the gender reveal but for the entire community. It'll bring everyone closer together and show how much we support one another."

Leah beamed, feeling overwhelmed with gratitude and joy. "I can't thank you both enough. This means the world to me."

"Well, you're family, Leah," Doris hugged her. "And this ranch is all about supporting and celebrating each other. We will make this the best ranch fair and gender reveal ever."

As they continued planning the event, the air was filled with anticipation and excitement.

Days turned into weeks, the preparations for the ranch fair and the gender reveal went full swing. Doris, Susan, Leah, and the rest of the residents worked tirelessly to ensure everything was perfect. Everyone was included; even Sarah, excited to be a big sister again, was bouncing around with extra energy as she was given different assignments to prepare for the shindig. In no time, the ranch was transformed into a fairground, buzzing with activity as decorations went up, stalls were set up, and new faces began to arrive to set up booths in anticipation of selling their wares.

On the day of the fair, the weather was perfect. The sun shone brightly, and a gentle breeze carried the sounds of laughter and the aroma of delicious food across the grounds. The fair was a lively event, with games, competitions, and activities for people of all ages. The lasso contest and the sack race were hits, and children delighted in the petting zoo filled with adorable farm animals.

A country band played upbeat tunes, and the dance floor was always full as people line-danced and twirled to the rhythm. The booths offered a variety of homemade goods, from jams and pies to handcrafted jewelry and art. The community had come together in a beautiful display of camaraderie and support, showcasing the heart of the ranch.

As the afternoon sun descended toward the horizon, anticipation for the gender reveal grew. A crowd gathered around the hay bale setup, where the sizeable decorated box sat on the hay wagon, ready to be hitched to a horse-drawn cart. The barrels labeled 'cowboys' and 'cowgirls' were nearly overflowing with votes, adding to the excitement.

Glowing with happiness, Leah stood beside Mike, Sarah, and young Bobby. She chose a lovely, flowing dress that accentuated her growing belly, and her face beamed joyfully.

"I can't believe this moment is finally here," she said, clutching Mike's hand.

"It's going to be perfect." He assured her, squeezing her hand back.

The horse-drawn cart, beautifully adorned with flowers and ribbons, approached, and Leah climbed onto the wagon with the help of Alphonse, who had come to show his support. The crowd hushed, a palpable sense of excitement filling the air.

"Are you ready, everyone?" Mike called out, his voice firm, quieting the crowd.

A resounding cheer erupted from the crowd. Leah took a deep breath, and together, she and Mike pulled the string. The box opened, and to everyone's surprise, a mix of blue and pink balloons floated into the sky. Gasps and murmurs of confusion rippled through the crowd.

Leah, laughing and crying simultaneously, turned to face everyone. "We have another surprise for all," she said, her voice shaking. "We're having twins! A boy and a girl!"

The crowd erupted into cheers and applause, the joyous news spreading like wildfire. Doris and Susan rushed to Leah, hugging her tightly as tears of happiness streamed down their faces. They each turned to Mike and hugged him, too, while Alphonse slapped him on his shoulder.

"Congratulations, Man!" he shouted above the noise of the crowd.

"This is the best surprise ever!" Susan exclaimed.

"We couldn't be happier for you," Doris added, her voice choked with emotion.

The rest of the evening was a whirlwind of celebration. The news of Leah's twins added a layer of joy to the fair, making it a day that no one would ever forget. The community danced, laughed, and celebrated late into the night, the stars twinkling overhead as a reminder of the miracles and blessings that life could bring.

As the fair wound down and people began to head home, Leah stood with Alice and Maria, watching the last guests leave.

"This day has been more than I could have ever dreamed," Leah said, her heart full.

Alice smiled warmly, her eyes reflecting the twinkling of string lights above them. "You deserve every bit of happiness, Leah. Seeing you so happy makes all the hard work worth it."

Maria nodded in agreement. "And to think, we were all in such different places just a few years ago. Now, look at us – part of something amazing, with so much to look forward to."

Leah glanced at her friends, her eyes brimming with tears. "I couldn't have done it without you both. Your support means the world to me."

Alice wrapped an arm around Leah's shoulders. "We're a family now, Leah. We stick together through thick and thin."

Maria grinned, adding, "And we've got two little ones to look forward to spoiling. It's going to be quite the adventure."

Leah laughed, feeling a surge of gratitude and love. "I can't wait to share every moment with you both. Here's to the future and our beautiful, ever-growing family."

The following day, as Leah was helping Doris and Susan clean up, she hugged them both, her emotions on edge from the previous day's events. "I can't thank you enough for everything," Leah said

"It's been our pleasure," Doris said, wrapping an arm around her. "You've brought so much joy to this ranch. We're just happy to share in your happiness."

Susan nodded in agreement, giving Leah a pat on her hand.

As the three women worked to tidy up, they looked out over the remains of the fairground and felt a deep sense of fulfillment and joy. The ranch had brought them together, and together, they had created something beautiful and lasting. The future looked bright, filled with promise and love, and they knew that whatever came their way, they would face it together as a family.

The End

Epilogue

One evening, Doris sat on her bed, reflecting on the past few months. She glanced at her calendar and realized that her wedding anniversary with Robert was approaching. She thought about all the milestones she had reached since saying goodbye to her beloved. It felt like a million miles away now. The sorrow was still there, and the loss would never truly heal. But she had found a reason to get up each morning. She had discovered a new life purpose beyond being Robert's wife. In this new purpose, she found a tranquility that she had never known before. She truly felt at peace.

That cold, dark day at the funeral seemed like a distant memory now, and sometimes, it all felt like a dream. The memories were bittersweet, a reminder of what she had lost but also a source of comfort and joy. With the promise of a new day ahead, Doris closed her eyes and dreamed of Robert with her on the ranch, riding horses and laughing as they galloped into the setting sun.

About the Author

Melissa Allred is a passionate author and stay-at-home mom with a talent for weaving compelling stories. With a heart for encouraging women in their faith. Melissa has written two books, The Princess and Her Owl and Hannah, that draw readers into the beauty and struggle of life. Her latest work, Hannah, explores the powerful story of a woman who yearned for a child and the incredible faith that sustained her through her darkest moments. As a homeschooling mother, Melissa understands the demands of busy family life and believes that everyone has a story worth telling. Through her writing, Melissa seeks to inspire her readers to live with hope, purpose, and faith.

Thank you for taking the time to learn more about me and my work. If you enjoyed reading Widow's Ranch and want to stay up-to-date on my future projects, I invite you to follow me on Substack: https://substack.com/@anointedinspired.

You can connect with me on:

🌐 https://substack.com/@anointedinspired

🔗 https://www.tiktok.com/@mallred5?_t=ZT-8s56OCNfQnz&_r=1

Subscribe to my newsletter:

✉ https://substack.com/@anointedinspired

Also by Melissa Allred

The Princess and her Owl

In the kingdom of Barinash, Princess Amrie was beloved by all. Her beauty, intelligence, and skill with a bow made her the envy of many. She lived a peaceful life with her father King Roland in their grand palace, but trouble was brewing in the kingdom.

Hannah

https://books2read.com/hannahfaith

A biblical fiction about Hannah and her journey through infertility and her faith. With a companion bible study

The Princess and her Owl: Adult Coloring book

After writing the Princess and her Owl, I saw that my son took an interest in the story. But he was not interested in my read it to him. So I condensed the novella down into tiny blurbs. And then I had the bright idea to make it into a companion to my Novella. Now adults and children alike can enjoy the book in an abridge version.

Renewed by Truth Album by: Anointed Inspired

This is not a book. It is a music album available to purchase from Apple and stream on Spotify as well Amazon Music.